UNPLUGGED

UNPLUGGED

Vol two

SIGAL EHRLICH

For Haven, I don't know you yet, but I already love you

CHAPTER One

CHAPTER

"Volunteering – our imbursement for living in this beautiful universe."
-A tattered plaque hanging in the volunteer camp kitchen.

I roll down the window and lean forward. Closing my eyes, I let the wind whip my cheeks and deeply inhale the icy chill. Riding up the mountain in the rusty, rickety truck sends my stomach to churn on every turn and twist as it crushes over the muddy, rough dirt road. I stare out the window, a wealth of heavy thoughts seizing my mind.

"Ivi, you're coming to the bonfire tonight?" Pedro, a Brazilian volunteer and my instant buddy, asks from the backseat, cutting off my contemplation.

I turn to give him a confirming nod followed by a thin smile. I met Pedro and his sister, Renata, the first day I got to the camp. They took it upon themselves to be my personal guides, what with their three days of seniority. Showing me around the village, they introduced me to the rest of the team – twenty awesome people from all corners of the globe. A delightfully diverse group of like-minded people who immediately make you feel welcome, happy, and most importantly, useful. All joined together, here in this small village which is both uniquely beautiful with its untamed nature and heartbreakingly damaged with its poverty and the destruction caused by the earthquake that recently hit. We have come together with one singular goal in mind: help make it better. It's not my first mission. I've been exposed numerous times to disasters and calamities that were both natural and manmade, yet, each time anew, my heart breaks all over again when I get to meet the people that essentially get to live the aftermath.

My nausea mollifies when the truck finally rolls to a stop at the site, near where we are lodged. A shabby, ragged stone house with a kitchen, if you can call an open cooking fire that, and more than a few small rooms for joined sleeping. It belongs to one of the village's teachers, miss Shristi. A diminutive older lady which funnily enough everyone calls Big Mom, who's always in colorful saris, with jingling bungles, a nose ring, a red bindi dot marking her forehead and an ever-present motherly smile. Renata, Pedro and I share a room on the second floor.

The driver, with a few missing teeth and a rolled cigarette held between his lips, walks over to the back of the car and drops down the tailgate. Pedro calls out for a couple of bulky guys to help him unload the truck and I join the rest of the group. I pull my work gloves out of my back pocket and take a few more steps, dodging downed trees' limbs, to reach Renata.

"Who's the new guy?" She tips her head at where her brother and the other guys unload log piles into a cart.

"There are two new guys, Re." I roll my eyes fondly at my gloves, shrugging them on. Every fresh day since we got here she's been interested in a different guy. Pedro once said that Renata believes she's in The Bachelorette rather than on a mission trip.

"The one with the incredible pecks and the wild blond curls."

I give surfer dude a glance and turn back to my friend. "Kenny. He's from England. You fancy?"

"Muito," she confirms in Portuguese, giving Kenny's rear too long of a stare to be considered innocent as he bends to drop yet another log to the cart.

Shaking my head, I link my arm in hers and tug her after me, toward the debris that once used to be a home of a lovely family of four. "Let's start this day, shall we? There'll be enough time to molest the poor boy at the bonfire."

Thus begins day eight of my mission trip.

Inhaling, I bend down to lift a large rock, my breath held with the exertion. By the eighth time I lift a heavy rock and walk over to set it in a cart, the process becomes almost robotic. Focusing on the music playing from my earbuds and the fresh, chilly air caressing my face, I ignore the smarting in my muscles and overall physical strain.

I halt with a block in my hands when I see Rajesh coming our way. Dropping the block back to the ground, I pull the earbuds out and smile at him. His big, dark eyes respond with amiability. His skinny arms flail as he hurries his steps toward me. "Hi Raj." I rub his shorn head, greeting him. The little boy's smile brightens, but his eyes with their perpetual glum don't match that sweet smile. They never do. He gestures at the smaller rocks and branches, signaling he's going to help us. Renata, who's a few steps away, and I share an emotional stare.

We've all temporarily adopted Rajesh. A sweet boy that's sometimes afraid to go home at night to his pimp daddy and house full of men he doesn't know. The loss of innocence surrounding this area is heartbreaking and hard to bear.

I watch Rajesh as he takes a candy bar from Renata with a shy smile and sigh with mild sadness. It's hard to accept, alas though, I know that some things, we, the volunteers, can't fix – perhaps this is the hardest part of being a volunteer – the exposure to things you just can't fix. I wipe my face with the back of my sleeve and resume removing debris.

Nine hours of clearing rubble from fallen houses and building the frame for two new ones. Some of us are already laying down concrete floors, and making the structure of wire, poles and bricks for the school they started working on a couple of weeks ago. An hour of break is all we take for food and drinks, otherwise it's hard work. Fulfilling work.

When four o'clock rolls in, there isn't a part in my body that doesn't protest. It's smarting all over from the physical exertion. I'm dirty and tired and exhausted but couldn't be more satisfied and content. Glancing at Big Mom's house, I cringe and decide to take a walk through the village instead. The house is by no means inviting or well insulated. Chilly breeze, insects and spiders enjoy cruising around the rooms as they please. We all try to spend as little time in them as possible, given the conditions. What a glaring contrast to my lodging conditions at Tyler's. Feels like I've been teleported to a completely different universe. Hard to believe these two realities coexist on the same globe.

Adjusting the earbuds in my ears, I hit shuffle on my playlist and begin my stroll. Chautara, in the Sindhupalchowk region, is one of the most devastated areas from the quake that hit nearly six months ago. The village is mostly self-reliant, with every spare piece of land used for crops of corn, fields of beans and chilies, grazing goats, buffalo and chickens with the occasional orange or apple tree. The scenery around the village is depressing. There's more than a lot of work to do to bring it back to an actual village condition. Just a few houses and a lone coffee shop made it through the devastation that rises up in piles upon piles of wreckage. But if you just lift your eyes a little higher, the glorious exquisiteness of the Himalayas subdues everything with its wild, powerful grace.

Taking the path to the forest with a soft tune playing in my ears, it's just me and my thoughts and immediately Tyler takes center stage. Every day that had passed since I've arrived in Nepal has empowered the assumption that the day Tyler brought me to the airport and told me he wanted to give us a try was a product of high emotions with little, if not zero thought behind them.

I can't deny the promise in his words, but it's one I'm having a hard time holding on to. It's hard to keep the hope alive when right up until this very moment, we haven't communicated. We never even agreed on the pragmatics of making anything between us work. We never agreed on anything to shift me coming back into motion. It was all up in the air. Nothing concrete to work with. Just like I ominously anticipated, when we parted ways over a week ago, it was a final good-bye rather than a promise for a reunion.

My musing make my heart feel a bit heavier as I walk through the peaceful, stunning nature.

Even though more than a week has passed, I still carry the weight of our good-bye. The thought of Tyler is still a constant flame in my head. This place has helped to lessen it into a low burning ember though. Breathtaking sunsets, spectacular nature and a wealth of misfortune and poverty is bound to do that to you. It knocked sense and reality into me in less than twenty hours after my arrival in Nepal.

My fountain of self-pity has been reduced to a drip. Real life and hardship have a tendency to minimalize, if not completely diminish, one's "little problems." If not put them to shame. It, if you will, smacks you upside the head, *hard*. Pummels some sense of perspective into you. Because really, what does a bruised heart in need of nursing have on a child begging to simply live?

Coming back, I find the team setting up the camp for dinner. Eva and Jana, two mid-fifties ladies from eastern Europe, help Big Mom with making the staple Nepali dishes, daal bhat and daal roti. Day in day out it's rice or flatbread with lentils, with the occasional twist on these meals with a few different styles of roti or rice pudding. If we're lucky, some potato and bean curry is served with the dish. It hasn't been that long since I set foot in this place and already the physical changes in my body are hard to miss. I'm more toned and my clothes feel a bit looser now.

I smile noticing Renata and Kenny setting up the wood for the bonfire. Both looking more than happy in each other's company. Bet he's getting a rose tonight.

I head to the hose attached to a nearby tree to freshen up. A bucket and a hose, Nepali style bath for you.

"Ivi." Big Mom's voice reaches me as I wash my face for the second time, rubbing my hands over it to get all the dirt out. Or at least try to. Hygiene, to say the least, is not exactly a priority here.

Drying my hands on my cargos, I walk over to meet her. "You called me?"

"You box." She says in her limited English with an encouraging smile.

My brows bunch as I try to decipher her words. "Do you need a box, Big Mom? Do you need me to put something in boxes?"

She shakes her head, her hoop earrings swaying with the movement. Her expression coils with frustration. "You box, room." A little triumphant smile curls her lips. "Package! You package room."

"There's a package in my room?" She grins at me with a nod. "A package for me?" I ask again. No one has ever sent me packages during any of my trips so far. Perhaps she's confusing me with one of the other volunteers.

"Package Ivi Kert." She says, reading my doubt. She drops her hands to either side of her hips, silently commanding acquiescence.

"Thank you." No point in arguing, Big Mom looks determined.

Indeed, on my narrow folding bed, on the itchy, tattered wool blanket stands a cardboard box with my name printed on a white label. Cautiously, I take the box in my hands for a closer look. Besides my name there is no other indications of what it is, or whom might have sent it. I bend to sit on the bed and put the box on my lap. My fingers itch to rip it open to find out what's inside. But they have nothing on my flipping belly and accelerated heart. I just know it. It's from him. It's from Tyler.

Shoving my hand in my thigh pocket, I feel for my swiss army knife. We all carry one around. With our current line of work and the general conditions, it's elementary. Flicking the blade up, I run it over the middle of the box, cutting through the tape. I flick the blade back in and pocket the knife. Biting on my lips, I push the box flaps to the sides.

A giggle escapes my mouth to the packs of peanut butter filled pretzels lining the box. There's a black cotton fabric nestled amid the snacks. Picking it up, I realize it's a folded shirt. I hold it up and let it roll down. Another chuckle leaves my mouth, this one louder. Joyful and amused to find Tyler's face plastered over the front, with a sexy smile. My own smile feels like it's coming straight from the center of my happy heart. I hug the soft fabric to my chest, and inhale. Longings wash over me with Tyler's scent hovering my nose. I close my eyes and inhale again. The thought of him thinking of spraying the shirt with his perfume just amplifies everything that sparking in me. When I turn to set the box aside with a dreamy smile and go join the rest of the group, I realize that there's something else at the bottom of the box. I cock my head looking at the smaller black box before opening it to reveal its content.

I observe the cell phone in my hand with its thicker body and funny looking antenna. And the penny drops. I've seen this type of phone before. It's a satellite phone. Tyler sent me a satellite phone. One of the only options to communicate with the outside world besides traveling to one of the surrounding cities which is at least sixty miles. That is if you're lucky enough to catch a ride there.

Besides being a source of communication to the world, I also know how pricey these calls are. I sigh, holding the phone between my hands. About to put it back in its box, I sense something attached to the back.

It's a little note folded in half, taped to the back. I release the paper and unfold it. I don't know what it is, but seeing Tyler's hand writing here, in this place, does things to me. Emotionally wonderful things.

Call me, Kiisu.

Three simple words that mean the world to me right now.

Giddy, I leave the room, not before tucking my care package under my backpack. Opting to call Tyler once I figure out the time difference (we're on two different continents, after all) I join my friends.

Both volunteers and some of the locals had congregated around the fire by the time I join. Kenny's friend, Billy, strums on a guitar while two of the older ladies in our group give a whole repertoire of The Beatles. The younger local crowd keep watching us like we're a new-found species. It's something you get used to quite quickly. They follow us a lot during the day. As a matter of fact, as soon as we leave the house, we have a small audience staring at us. Especially those of us from Northern European descend. The fairer you are, the most fascinated looks and followers you get.

I walk over to help myself to some Chiya, a local tea with milk. Noticing Mike approach, a proud American veteran with whom I had an immediate click, I remain in my place. Cradling the metal mug with both hands I bring it closer to my mouth and blow on it, waiting for Mike.

"Ivi." Mike tips his head, reaching for the thermos.

I grab a mug and hold it out for him to pour the steaming tea. "Erm, Mike, do you happen to know what the time difference between Nepal and the states is?"

Taking the full mug from me, Mike asks, "Where in the states, darling?"

"Oh." It takes me some beats to answer, because I don't have one.

I know that Tyler is on a mini tour across the states, but I have no idea where he might be right now. "LA?" Comes out as a question rather than an answer.

Taking a sip of his tea, Mike licks his lips. "Nepal is about fourteen hours ahead of LA." Mike's mouth twitches as my mind drifts, doing the math. "It should be around six a.m. in the City of Flowers and Sunshine."

I give him a self-effacing smile, which he returns with an amicable one. With our steaming mugs in hand, talking about the progress we made today, we walk toward the group. I share a boulder with Pedro who brought us each a dish of daal roti. With a tummy full of warm, wholesome food and a content, easy smile, I watch the people around me, feeling utterly blessed to be a part of the group. Familiar tunes have me slice my stare to Kenny who's holding the guitar now, crossed-legged on the floor beside us. Longings explode in my stomach when he sings one of Tyler's songs. I hug myself, watching him, listening and counting the minutes till I make that phone call.

When the logs turn into burning coals and people start to scatter for the night, I volunteer to do the dishes. A way to keep myself occupied till another hour passes and it won't be as early in LA.

At ten, with my phone in hand, I make it to one of the swings suspended from a sturdy ficus with aerial roots. To a moon lit corner, away from the house. Away from the few who remain outside to chat and smoke. With a shaky hand, I dial Tyler's number. The ringing sound has my stomach coil with anticipation like a tight spring.

In lieu of a greeting Tyler says, "I've dreamt about you nearly every night since you left." His voice surges right to my heart. He sounds tired and weary. His voice distinctively hoarse, not his usual husky cadence, like it was overly used, strained. But the emotions it brings, the butterflies it releases inside me. The sweet press on my chest.

Though all I want is to tell him that I missed him so much I could hardly breathe, I downplay it, going with a tease instead. "Is that a new sappy song?"

Tyler chuckles. I can hear something clicking at his teeth, and then a deep swallow. "No, it's literally how my nights have gone since you left me." Another clink and a swallow. Probably the herb candy he chews on whenever he's strained his vocal cords.

"Are you after a concert?"

He hums a confirmation, "Yep, last night."

"How did it go?"

He chuckles briefly after a short pause. "There were a few thousand calling my name and the only one I wanted next to me is far away."

"Where's that person? Can't you, I don't know, do the thing you do. Flick your fingers and have someone bring that person to you?"

"Can't do that, she's too busy saving the world." His voice brims with flirtation. His chuckle is an afterthought. "I don't want to upset the universe. You know what they say, Karma's a bitch and all that." After another short pause, he adds in a low voice, clear of tease, "Ivi, I meant what I said before you left."

My chest feels heavier.

"And now after not seeing you, or talking to you for over a week, I'm more than certain. Come back."

"Needy, are we?" I joke, too overwhelmed to tell him I'm moments away from throwing everything to hell and jumping on the next plane out to LA. My soft chuckle dies to the extended silence on the line. "Tyler … you're quiet." I break the silence in a soft chord.

He takes a generous inhale. "Yeah." Then, "I'm waiting for you to really hear me." He exhales audibly. "Really listen to what I'm trying to say. I want to give us a chance, Ivi."

"I'm listening, Tyler." It's a choked whisper.

"I feel like I haven't been the same since the morning after … you.

You're everywhere. All over my mind. All the more since you left."

"Tyler —"

He cuts me off before I'm able to say another word. "Ivi." He brings my wayward thoughts to a screeching halt. "It's simple, very simple, as I see it. What we had is too good to not at least give it a chance. It's about two people liking each other. That's it. I want you to come back and move back in."

Move back in? I thought … I don't know what I thought. But this is… "Are you serious right now?"

"The boxes you asked Eli to send to Estonia. I asked him not to. They are here, waiting for you."

"You are serious," I say on an incredulous breath.

"Yeah, I am. Come back to me, Kiisu."

It seems like we talk for hours. My eyelids become heavy, and goosebumps cover my skin. Chill descends upon the night and I'm shivering, but I don't want to hang up. Tyler's voice soothes me like a warm bath and soft blankets.

"Ivi?" Concern rims his question. "It sounds like you're shivering."

"I might be a tiny bit cold," I say and let out a choked sneeze. "As in completely frozen."

"Get inside. Go to bed. Call me tomorrow."

"Tyler?"

"Mmmhmm."

"Everything you said before." My voice comes out softer. "I feel the same way."

"Night Kiisu." It's tender and quiet and full of everything I want to hear. "See you when I fall asleep."

See you when I fall asleep. Euphoric rush prevents me from falling asleep long after Tyler tells me those sweet, sweet words. I hug my pillow, filled to a brim by thrill.

Tyler and I are happening …

When my book, my thoughts, and even the one and only Sleep with Me podcast doesn't do the job of transferring me into slumber realm, I give up. Instead, I grab one of the peanut butter pretzel bags in Tyler's care package and dive into it like a ravenous raccoon.

CHAPTER
Two

"Love. Many translations, one universal intention."
A framed quote in the sole coffee shop in the village.

"Do you have a thing for Kenny?"

There's some energetic conversation buzz in the background, which to me is white noise. I'm floating in Tyler Land, snippets from our last few good calls boosting my happy. Due to his busy tour schedule and the time difference we don't get to talk every day, but each time we do, it lifts my happy a little higher. I miss him even more with each call.

"Do you?" I finally realize that Renata is talking to me.

"What?" I ask, tearing my stare from where it wandered to while my mind took a tour down infatuation lane. My brows crinkle when the spot my eyes were honed in on becomes clearer. Kenny, who my stare got stuck on, gives me a toothy grin from a couple of tables away.

"You do, don't you!" Renata deflates.

I spin to look at her. "What, no!"

She raises an incredulous brow. "Re-al-ly?" She stretches the three syllable word, her accent softening the R. "Could have fooled me...you were, you know, ogling him *for the last ten minutes* with silly, googly eyes."

"I spaced out. Believe me, I'm not interested in Kenny." Or anyone else on earth for that matter. Who could even stand a chance next to Tyler?

She gives me another assessing scan before turning to her brother. "What do you say?"

He nods, taking a sip of his coffee, then adds, "You kind of been walking around with this goofy smile and crazy, dreamy eyes since last week. Enamorada ... seriously crushing." As though that tidbit somehow corroborates Renata's suspicion.

"Well, there's a good explanation for that. There's this ..." How do I even begin to describe Tyler? Boy? Definitely not. Man? More like it, but still, sort of rings too adulty in my head. Guy? I guess. Yet it seems way too simple for Tyler. "A guy, um — friend, I guess, that — we used to have a thing. Well, he reached out to me last week, and I think we're, um ... I guess, back together?" The tail end of my answer rings of uncertainty. Hearing "back together" leave my mouth immediately brings back the silly smile my friends accused me of just seconds ago.

Renata grins, squinting at her brother conspiringly. "Oh, Mr. Ca-ching!"

"Excuse me?" Shoots out of my lips.

"He's the one who sent you that phone, isn't he?"

I huff, slumping in my seat. Looking around the shabby coffee shop, I try to figure out how to explain Tyler. I'm not too inclined on discussing ... him. Nor, do I know how to even begin explaining him. I want to laugh, thinking that they probably won't even believe me if I went with the simple truth.

"Yeah. He's the guy who sent me the care package."

Renata frowns, looking at her brother again. Her stare, somewhat tentatively, crawls back to me. "Who's this guy, why would he send you a Tyler Lee Adams shirt?"

"Pardon?" My brows nearly reach my hairline. "You went through my stuff?"

"Hey, no need to get all offensive. It wasn't exactly like that. Well, it was sort of open and I might have pushed it a little to open it wider." She gives me a bashful smile and flings her pointer finger in a little push gesture.

"Don't make that cute face. It's not helping," I say. We have zero privacy in our little room as it is, please don't go through my stuff, okay?"

"Sorry, it won't ever happen again." She has the decency to look a little repentant while crossing her heart. For a second and a half that is. Her lips curve up. "It was truly tempting." Before I'm able to scold her again, she quickly adds, "So what's the story with the shirt."

I generally don't lie. At least try not to. A white lie once every blue moon, maybe. Especially for the benefit of the other person. I bite on my lip, looking at the sediments of tea in the bottom of my mug. A lie of omission is still a lie, but, *oh well*. "He knows I'm a huge admirer of Tyler Lee Adams' music." I slowly raise my eyes to a wide grin.

"Dios Mio." She fans herself theatrically. "That man is so hot!"

I wince. Not the greatest fan of Renata swooning over Tyler. "He's a great singer," I say flatly, opting to move on to the next subject.

"When this idiota was younger," Pedro rolls his eyes his sister's way, "She used to kiss his posters."

Cringing, I try to divert the narrative. "So, what's the latest on Kenny?"

Soon I learn that Kenny is great, but so is Aksel from Denmark. Pedro and I trade amused glances with the following subtext: Renata is back to her old antics.

"Ta bom." Okay, Pedro announces twenty minutes later. "It's our turn to clean the house today, my ladies. Shall we?" He gestures toward the door of the café — the beads curtain leading to the street.

Cleaning Big Mom's house is one of my least favorite tasks around here. It comes tight with taking an outdoor shower and rubble clearing. No matter how much you scrub, wipe or swipe, it always looks the same. Shabby sans the chic part. Yet, taking it in stride, we all do it in turns.

Absorbed in scrubbing the heck out of the kitchen counter, I jolt a little when the phone vibrates in my thigh pocket. Wiping my hands on my pants, I fetch the device out. Both my lips and heart smile when I read the message.

Tyler: Call you in an hour?

So. Much. Yes.

I text back. At the end of our first phone call, I decided to let go of my hesitations. Encouraged by Tyler's enlightening openness with how he feels about me, I decided to not hold back either.

Two minutes later another text lands in my phone.

Tyler: Serious issue, Kiisu ...

A beat later as I'm about to send a reply, a new text follows.

Tyler: Can't stop thinking about you.

Butterflies go wild in my stomach.

———•———

A duet of rain and wild winds keep pelting the windows, deviously gusting in an icy breeze. With one candle lit in the center of our room, Renata, Pedro and I, bury under all our blankets combined. We squeeze against each other in Pedro's narrow bed, where we lodged right after the light had been cut off, curtsy of the storm wreaking havoc outside.

"I will never survive this weather. We're from Brazil, we don't do real winter," Renata says through chattering teeth. "This is it, this is how I'm going to die. Que triste." *How sad* she adds in her mother tongue. Turning to her brother, she says, "Don't ever let mamãe read my diary when I'm gone." Which prompts a long and hilarious banter between the siblings.

When their amicably poking at each other marathon subsides, they each tell me about what awaits them at home when they leave in less than two weeks. Pedro will return to his longtime girlfriend and third year in med school. Renata to her dancing/bartending "career" and to a wealth of debauchery as her brother puts it.

"What about you?" Pedro asks me next.

"I'll be going back to the states, for ..." For what? For how long? God, that even sounds crazy in my head. How can I explain it to someone else when *I* don't even have a clear answer? "To visit with friends. For a while."

"And then?" Renata prompts.

"Full honesty, guys—" I shrug, gaping at the droplets dancing wildly on the steamed window. "I have no idea."

They both look at me skeptically. "Um, well," My phone, ringing from my bed stops me from trying to explain to my friends, and myself, what I'm doing. Jumping out of our little human cauldron, I answer the call. "Hi," my voice mellows on cue to Tyler's "Hey."

"Did you catch that?" Pedro asks Renata, his eyes trained on me.

Mirroring her brother, Renata says, "Wow, she's got it bad."

Turning my back halfway, opting for some sort of privacy, I resume trying to listen to Tyler on the other line. The phone signal is pretty poor indoors, but with the storm blazing outside ... I have no other choice but to stay in and endure the bad reception and my friend's prying eyes and attentive ears. I walk to stand by the window.

"Tyler, I can't hear you too well, you're cutting out," I tell Tyler, when something he tried to tell me about Jeremy reaches me in broken sentences.

"Ivi?" Tyler's voice sounds metallic just before the line cuts us off.

"So, lover boy's name is Tyler? Eh." Pedro teases.

"Just like Tyler Lee Adams, what a coincidence. Did you hook up with him because of his name?" Renata giggles amused with her little jab.

"You guys are really bored, ah?" I say, not letting them go any further. "Now, scoot over, I'm freezing."

The room lights up with sporadic lightning and the walls eco with angry thunder, carrying us through the next hour with light conversation and silly sibling banter. Around midnight when our yawns become frequent and our voices heavy with fatigue, we each scatter to our own bed. About to set my phone on the floor next to my bed, an incoming text prompts it to flicker.

> **Tyler: The press found out about Jeremy. My people are handling it. Kid's taking it in stride.**

I try to text him back, but the bad connection prevents my reply from ever leaving my phone.

———•———

I look around me. Pedro and Renata are busy contemplating what to order in this charming, little Internet café we're at. It's located in a neighboring town to which we had to drive over an hour this morning. A well-deserved hiatus from our hard work. Finally, a place where my laptop can come in use and most importantly a genuine way to connect to the cyber world. It's the first time in nearly three weeks that we have left the village. A stolen morning to replenish on basic necessities among other much needed "services." Renata and I splurged on some beauty treatments. The situation under our shabby appearance wasn't much better than the exterior. Plucked, waxed and pampered, I lean back in the chair and scroll through my phone for the fifth time in less than ten minutes.

Time difference sucks! Big time.

I'm practically itching to dial Tyler's number after getting a bunch of text messages that didn't come through last night. And the photos he sent me. The photos!

With my friends still busy ordering nearly every available dish on the menu, I can immerse myself in my screen with a silly smile on my face. I send the pictures to my email to look at them on my laptop. For the bigger screen of course. And oh Lord, the warm tremor cruising through me, twirling in my stomach. I'm mesmerized, studying Tyler's face as he smiles at me with a quaint smile, his brown eyes flirting with me from under his lashes. My eyes trail to the message on my phone.

Tyler: Hope you weren't too emotionally attached to my hair.

With a soft smile controlled by my swooning heart, my eyes draw back to the photo on my screen where Tyler rubs his shortly cropped hair, looking at me with a boyish smile. I turn back to the second photo he sent me and my smile widens while I let out a tender sigh. Tyler and Jeremy both smiling widely at me with a matching buzz cut. Tyler's arm is swung around Jeremy's neck, their temples touching.

A photo that Tyler captioned with: **It's for a good cause ...**

I can't take my eyes off his face. He looks younger, his masculine features enhanced now, lacking the frame of his hair which somehow gave them a softer edge. He's stunning. Seeing him like that, with Jeremy, both smiling at me, longing overflows me. I'm giddy, wishing I could call him now, but it's too early. Way too early on his side of the pond, and with him still touring, I know his nights are exhausting and how much he needs his rest. Pedro, pulling a chair next to me, has me minimizing the photos on my screen to give him my attention.

Renata joins us a moment later, setting a few breakfast dishes in the center of our table. After small talk and a whole lot of munching, they both set their own electronic devices on the table and we continue talking while catching up on everything we missed, being isolated from the real world for over three weeks now.

After answering a few emails and catching up on my friends' lives via social media, I do something that I haven't done since that one time I looked up info about Tyler having a kid. I stalk him online. A baffling experience, if I may. I might be more than a bit overwhelmed by the number of hashtags associated with Tyler. With Tyler's hair, Tyler's smile, Tyler's eyes, Tyler's voice, I wouldn't be surprised if there's a hashtag for Tyler's flossing routine. The last two, the most trending ones, #TylerLeeAdamsSocks and #TylerLeeAdamsSon, direct me to the world of Twitter. Worrying my lips out of pure curiosity, I skim through the flood of speculations about Jeremy. *I hope he handles it well.* We haven't spoken about it yet, but I'm more than positive Tyler will do everything he can to make sure Jeremy remains unscathed. As much as one can while being thrown into public attention, en masse.

Engrossed and somewhat amused, I look up the #TylerLeeAdamsSocks hashtag. A giggle escapes my mouth just before I cover it with my hand. The brief amusement is a product of the many retweets of a photo Tyler apparently posted a couple of days after Christmas. The image shows Tyler's legs clad in worn jeans stretched before him next to a fireplace with my Christmas gift, the socks I made him as the focal point of the photo. My lips stretch even wider to his caption and fall open when I read the full tweet. I'm left stunned.

@TylerLeeAdams: Best. Christmas. Gift. Ever.

The next image is of a woman, also posted by Tyler, the woman's hair covers her face, revealing only her serine smile. My heart pauses and right after, melts.

@TylerLeeAdams: This, and her smile.

It's a candid photo of me, I'm unrecognizable, but that sedated, dreamy smile, definitely belongs to me. And it brings me back to lying next to the fire, next to Tyler, on one of the most memorable nights of my life.

CHAPTER
Three

"I'll hold you in my heart until I can hold you in my arms." -Peter Pen.
A quote from a favorite childhood book Ivi started rereading last night.

"Hey." His voice alone makes my body come alive. It baffles me each time anew, how powerful his effect is on me. Like I'm under a constant spell. In a dreamy, euphoric Tyler-enchantment.

"Tere." *Hi*, I say in Estonian. To be precise, I purr it like a little kitten. God, I got it so ridiculously bad.

"Tere, Kiisu." Tyler's voice is low and flirtatious.

"So, what do you — " Him.

"Tell me everything about — " Me.

Our questions collide and morph into low, goofy chuckles.

"You go first," Tyler says, ever the gentleman, which he insists he's not.

"How's Jeremy handling being," I laugh dryly. "Outed."

Tyler chuckles briefly. "I think he kind of enjoys the attention. Though I managed to control it in a way. Eli gave a bland statement to appease the tabloids. Something to prevent them from starting to dig further." As an afterthought, he adds in a pleased tone, "Fans been pretty cool about it." A muffled sound of rustling sheets reaches me when he pauses. My mind, as a reflex, conjures an image of Tyler in bed, prompting a heated flutter beneath my navel. His next words come out dripping sarcasm. "Comes with the job; people expect me to produce the occasional scandal, or sensation. Guess no one's really shocked."

"And finally, you throw them a crumb!" I declare and add, "If we're being honest here, I must say that your feigned choir boy act of late has been sort of boring." I tease, my chuckle soft. "Imagine the headlines if they ever found out that their idol has been slumming, *shnoodling* the hired help!"

"Shnoodling." Tyler murmurs through a snort. "Fuck, you think someone would spill the beans about Adina and I ... shnoodling?"

"Ha, ha," I say drily while grinning to myself.

Tyler goes on and recounts the highlights of Jeremy becoming "public knowledge." I laugh fondly when he spices it up with some of Jeremy's trademark gems. My favorite is the one where the boy read somewhere how celebrity parents impact baby name statistics and he can't wait for a new generation of Jeremys to arrive in the world.

"So?" Tyler says fifteen minutes into our call.

"So?" I echo.

His voice reaches me with an amused lilt. "There were people who got personally offended, some loved it, and more than a few even mourned the loss of my hair."

I snort in amusement. Oh, Tyler's almighty locks.

"And yet, you haven't reacted to it," he continues.

"Oh, you cut your hair? I knew there was something different about you, I just couldn't put my finger on it."

A breathy chuckle comes from the other line.

I bite on my lip. "I think you look very sexy with your buzz cut Mr. Adams." *I can't wait to run my fingers over it. Can't wait to see it up close.*

To feel it against my skin.

"Glad you approve, Miss Kert."

Then Tyler goes on and explains how the sensational haircut came to be. That Jeremy's school had a fundraiser event to raise awareness for children's cancer research, where both Jeremy and Tyler got their hair shaved. A gesture that raised a hefty sum. With an affectionate tone, Tyler adds, "Like a champ, Jeremy stepped up and got his own head shaved." Pride and genuine adoration fills me as I imagine them both going through the noble deed.

"I'm sorry Tyler, but I think your son is the real rock star."

"Nothing to apologize for, Kiisu. Couldn't agree more."

The sun is set low in the sky as we make it back to camp. I claim a moment to take in the glorious vision in front of me, telling my friends that I'll catch up with them shortly. I take a deep breath and drink in the breathtaking mountains now shining with soft pink-gold, caressed by the late-noon sun. The chilled air enhanced by freshness of open lands and greens fills my lungs. The scenery in this untamed part of the world is like none other, yet what lies beneath it is so devastating and wounded. I turn around to look at the village. The hard work we've put in thus far is noticeable, but there's still so much to do. We can fix the living conditions. The material things are simpler to restore. What we can't fix are the bruised human lives scathed by misfortune and injustice.

Holding on to the thought of our accomplishments so far and of what is waiting for me after this mission trip, I collect my thoughts and go join my team for a status update now taking place in Big Mom's living room.

I listen to Mike talk about progress and deadlines, nodding, making my best effort not to let the bitter-sweet feeling larking in the back of my mind to distract me. Mike explains that the initial workload assumption was wrong which caused for the delay with completing our work on the school we're rebuilding. "A delay of thirty days, give or take a few," Mike concludes, nodding at one of the older ladies.

I purse my lips. I really wanted to be here when the school reopened. To be here and finally feel like I've done something to help, done something to alleviate, at least a small bit, the suffering. Be here when the kids come into a new place with the new toys and equipment people donated. I wanted to be here just for a glimpse of their faces when they get to see everything that we're preparing for them.

Well, that won't happen. I can't afford coming back so soon. I need to save some money first. Another thought that starts an entirely different tailspin in my mind. What the heavens am I going to do when I'm back in the states besides canoodling with my… with Tyler?

CHAPTER
Four

CHAPTER

"You want to make God laugh, tell him your plan."
A quote by Woody Allen Ivi read (and snorted sarcastically over)
just before boarding her flight..

"Ladies and gentlemen, the captain has turned on the fasten seatbelt sign. We are now crossing a zone of turbulence. Please return to your seats and keep your seatbelts fastened. Thank you." When the inflight announcement ends with a static purr, I check my seatbelt and gaze out the round window. Knowing full-well that the best way to pass the long hours that follow is by sleeping, I still can't seem to relax and let the plane's hum lull me to sleep. It's rather incredible how a few hours and a couple of miles above the clouds can disconnect you from one reality and sends you off to a completely different one.

Just a few hours ago, I hugged my friends goodbye with promises to keep in touch and a hope to meet again someday. Departing from most of the team was easier than the intimate, emotional goodbye from Renata, Pedro, and not to mention, Raj.

Pedro is going back to Brazil in a week. Renata decided to stay for another month. Just like me, she wanted to be there when the school reopens. Only she'll get to do that and I won't. As Pedro put it, "One call to daddy and she gets to stay."

Leaving Raj was a different story, though. Familiar with his living conditions and what he faces daily, the crack in my heart with his name on it splits a little wider. All these people I get to meet on my mission trips are like threads twirling around a spool that's located inside of me, little by little cushioning, enriching me with their life stories, personalities and uniqueness. Making the spool bigger and tighter, fuller with unique experiences I get to live and special people I'm lucky enough to meet. Forever they'll have a special place in me, all of them.

"Miss, what would you like to drink?" The flight attendant stands by my row with a kind smile, one hand loose on the trolley.

"Tomato juice, please." I order the one drink people order *only* on flights.

"Anything else?" She serves me the drink with a little napkin.

"I'm good. Thank you."

Bringing the drink to my lips, I watch in complete horror as the glass shakes in my hand and a splash of liquid tomato sloshes back out, tainting my white cotton shirt and the triangle between my thighs in puréed red. Of course it would happen with tomato juice! It's not enough that normal people like myself usually look like they've emerged from the eye of a hurricane after a transatlantic flight. Now I get to meet the man of my dreams looking like I've been shot in the stomach and … a bit lower.

Getting back from the toilet with the stains somewhat faded yet still noticeable, I plop into the seat with an annoyed sigh. The thought of seeing Tyler in a few long hours not in an entirely pristine condition, to say the least, quickly snowballs into bigger concerns. I'm heading to L.A. again. This time around I have no real purpose or plan. I'm about to put my life on hold just to be with someone. Little by little, I'm freaking myself out. What am I doing? It feels like my rationale and sensibility barometer is out of whack, making me giddy. I'm venturing back to be with Tyler with no other direction whatsoever. No grand plan. No clue as to what's next.

No, really? What. Am. I. Doing?

I take a deep breath and put thoughts of consequences and repercussions in a provisional "fudge that" pile, plunge my earbuds in, close my eyes, and let this red-eye flight take me to my next destination. Take me to Tyler.

———————— ♦ ————————

After a quick stop at the toilets where I try, once more, to rid my clothes of the pinkish smudges, I make my way to baggage claim. I'm starting to think that maybe the universe is trying to send me a message as I gape at the abandoned conveyer belt, lamely rotating a single torn bag tag.

By the time I'm done filling out forms and going over the missing baggage procedure with the brisk agent, my exasperation reaches new heights. I apologize for snapping at the now scowling agent, take my documents and head toward the arrivals hall. The thought of seeing Tyler soon both soothes me, like I'm coming back home, and adds a new kind of anxiety, only this one involves an urge to rush to the closest bathroom and vomit. Taking a few more steps, I look for Victor, Tyler's driver. I burst out into laughter when I spot him. My tension dissipates at once. Standing tall, a head above everyone around, with a fitted black suit and his perpetual frown, Victor holds up a whiteboard boasting "*KIISU*" in bold black marker.

He nods when he sees me, advancing my way. "Welcome back, Miss Kert." He scans me solemnly. His brows pinch. "No luggage?"

"It got lost," I say on a sigh, feeling a bit out of place, having a private driver pick me up… especially looking like I do. Next to him, in his crisp suit and impeccably ironed dress shirt, I look like a runaway teen. "Tore, just tore," I mumble to myself. That's how I'm going to meet Tyler soon.

"They are running late. They haven't left New York yet." As we make our way to the car, Victor informs me that Tyler is not waiting for me in the car, or at home, like I hoped he would.

My gloomy spirit drops a little lower. Victor opens the back door for me, waiting as I get in.

When he settles in the driver's seat and cranks the car, I clear my throat and ask, "Victor, would you mind dropping me off somewhere else?"

Looking a tad uncomfortable with my request, he says, "Mr. Adams said to take you — "

"It's okay, I'll talk to Tyler when he's back." Not allowing him any space for debate, I give him the new address.

———— ◆ ————

"Hey … what a surprise! Come here, you."

Jay's arms around me are like salve to my weariness.

"Didn't think I'd get to see you so soon, thought Ty wouldn't let you out of sight," he murmurs as though to himself.

I burrow under his embrace for some long soothing moments before letting the poor guy I just dropped on unannounced, go.

"You look like an adorable train wreck." He gives me an elated grin.

"Thanks, I guess," I murmur and add, "I feel like I've just been through one."

"Want to freshen up?" he suggests. Giving me another look, he says. "Grab a shower?"

"Please. That would be wonderful."

He points to the hall. "Last room on the left."

Taking a couple of steps, I turn back to face him. "Um, do you have anything I can borrow, my clothes are a total mess."

He gives me another look and nods. "Sure." Less than a minute later, Jay offers me a bundle of folded clothes and a towel. "Here, make yourself un-stinky!"

———◦———

"I swear, you're like my private fairy godmother," I tell Jay, cradling the mug with herbal tea he made me while I was in the shower.

"I'd feel more comfortable with a less feminine label, thank you very much," he counters.

"My savior," I say in a ridiculously low, masculine tone.

Jay chuckles briefly. "You sound like you might be suffering from constipation."

That earns a throw pillow in the face.

Grinning, Jay plops next to me on the sofa and extends his legs on the coffee table. His grin turns mischievous as he turns to face me. "So, you're back."

"That I am." I set the teacup beside me and burrow my palms inside the long sleeves of Jay's borrowed hoodie.

He keeps his dancing eyes on me. "Lookie, Lookie, little miss Kert is about to play house with *the* Tyler Lee Adams."

"Playing house." My murmur comes out in perfect harmony to my eye roll.

Jay's grin doesn't waver. "What else should I call it?" Jay brings his pointer finger forward. "Living together, check." He touches his other pointer finger to the one he has outstretched. "Coupling. Check." Another confirming finger gesture follows. "A kid. Check."

"Okay. Ha ha. Not funny." I point up my finger. "Living together, not sure. Check." I tap my other finger to my pointed one. "Kid's not mine. Check. Got my point?" I frown at him amicably.

Disregarding my little play of defiance, Jay brows wrinkle. "What do you mean by living together, not sure. Ty knows about this? Because as far as I understood, you moving back in was a given."

I lightly shake my head. "I don't know." I gaze ahead. "It's not like I'll be working for Tyler now. I need to — " I huff. "I don't know what I need." I sigh. "Find my own place, find a job, settle in, you know ..." It's more of a question rather than an answer. Questions I've began asking myself ever since I insisted I purchase my own ticket back to the states. A long and almost futile battle. "I guess this is something I need to figure out by myself."

Our conversation gradually moves on to less stressing topics: Jay's work, someone he had two and a half dates with, my trip to Nepal, Max's latest antics and a new Thai food place Jay insists we should visit together. When my eyes become heavy, Jay encourages me to stay awake, fight the jetlag. Albeit, as the minutes tick by there's only so much I can do to stay awake. Powerful fatigue takes over and in no time, I snuggle against the armrest and cease fighting it.

———◆———

"What do you mean?" A low voice tainted by exasperation penetrates my deep slumber.

"Hey, don't look at me." I blink my eyes open to Jay spreading his arms sideways, transmitting: "not my fault."

Blinking away sleep, my eyes hone in at the scene before me where Jay is shrugging to a solemn Tyler. *Tyler!* Seeing Tyler a few feet away has my heart skip a beat or seven. Thirty days of longing. Thirty days of wanting him so bad, and he's here, right in front of me. I inch up, clearing my voice, "Tyler?"

Feels like my voice has the same effect on him as his presence has on me. As though shaken out of a dream he turns to me, his expression a mixture of sweet surprise and excitement. With eyes caressing the sight of me, Tyler closes the distance between us.

I watch him raptly, drinking in every bit of his handsome self, from his new shorn head to the charcoal blazer over white t-shirt, to his destressed jeans, down to the army boots on his feet while my heart slams wildly against my ribcage.

Reaching me, he crouches to level our stares. The most tender smile dons his bristle coated lips just before he leans in to softly kiss my lips. "Tere, Kiisu."

A happy, timid smile stretches my lips. "Tere, Tyler."

Still looking at me like I'm the most precious thing in the universe, Tyler sends his palm to cup my cheek. "God, I missed you," he says and surprises me as he pulls me into a tight hug.

"So, I guess I'm not needed here anymore," Jay says over a teasing grin.

Easing back from our embrace, I rise to stand. "Thank you for everything." I send Jay a thankful smile. My eyes meet the window that reveals a pitch dark night. "What time is it?"

"After two," they answer in stereo.

Here's to fighting the jet leg. I've slept for a good two hours.

"What are you wearing?" Tyler's voice calls for my attention. His brows bunch, eyes scanning me. I return his quizzical gaze. "I was a total mess after the flight and Jay was kind enough to lend me his shower and some clothes."

It's my turn to give Tyler a perplexed look, what with the frown furrowing his features and the little muscle working under his jaw.

Taking my hand in his, Tyler turns to Jay, "We'd better be going." I jerk my head back in surprise to his weird change of air.

Clearly amused by Tyler's sudden testiness, Jay nods, a secretive smile decorating his lips as if he's on to some intel he finds entertaining. "Sweet dreams, Grumpbunny." Nodding at me, he adds, "Night, Ivi."

I let go of Tyler's hand and step over to hug Jay. "Thanks, I'll talk to you tomorrow."

———◆———

For a few long minutes into the drive to Tyler's, I let the dust settle over whatever came over my private beloved enigma, who's now absorbed on the road ahead. A few long minutes in I try very hard not to jump to the conclusion that his sudden withdrawal has something to do with me. But the intrusive thought of, perhaps now that I'm finally here … I'm not that appealing, torments me. Just like a long lost toy that you miss while it's gone, but once you find it … it's nice to have but quickly loses its appeal. Five minutes is about as long as I can hold my tongue before breaking the silence. "Earth to Tyler," I say through a little grin, eyes hesitantly gauging his reaction.

Snapping out of his brooding, Tyler gives me a sidelong glance. His own mouth curves into a smile when he notices mine. He sends his hand to link his fingers with mine. Squeezing it once, he brings our joint hands to his mouth. Gently grazing his lips against my palm, he says to my skin, "I'm so glad you're here."

I let out an inward sigh of relief. "Glad to be here." On a lower chord, I add, "With you."

Tyler's eyes, dark and intense, leave the road to look at me. Breaking our eye lock, he throws a glance at the rear-view mirror, another quick one at the windshield and in one swift move swerves sharply onto the graveled shoulder and stops. In the same urgent fashion as he brought the car to a stop, he yanks off the seatbelt and turns to me. His hands haste to frame my face. For a stilled beat, holding my face in his large hands, he wordlessly stares at me. And then he leans in and kisses me. Kisses me like he can't stop himself, like he needs me to stay alive.

Soft moans of need funnel through our meshed mouths as Tyler releases my seatbelt and pulls me over to sit on his lap, his lips never leaving mine. Everything inside me quivers as we take turns in dominating the kiss. Tyler's hands find their way under my shirt to my waist and mine band around his neck.

In no time, we forget where we are. Utterly consumed in each other, our innocent kissing devolves into almost full-on exhibitionism. With his lips hovering over my exposed chest and his hands making their way inside the back of my pants, Tyler says my name, "Ivi." It doesn't sound lustful but rather a call for my attention.

Shamelessly grinding over him, with my own hands on his bare abs, eyes closed in bliss, I hum an incoherent response. "Mm."

"Ivi." It's a bit harsher this time.

I snap my eyes open to find Tyler frowning while reluctantly adjusting my shirt, covering me.

Clearing his throat, looking utterly deliciously disheveled, he says, "A car just stopped next to us, and you know … paparazzi, I don't want to risk — "

"God." I jolt to straighten on his lap, adjusting my shirt tighter around me, eyes wider than humanly possible.

Tyler chuckles, his dimple joins the merriment. "Not that I mind showing you off to the world, but I'd be damned if I let anyone see you so damn wanton, or your gorgeous tits."

My instant blush in response to his words feels a bit prudish following the brazen grinding and kissing.

The little smirk tickling Tyler's lips, I'm pretty sure, is a product of my sudden bashfulness. "Let's go home. I need to do this properly." His concluding kiss is a prelude for things to come.

———— ◆ ————

Tyler shuts the door behind us and all of a sudden the familiar foyer of his home feels different, maybe even a little intimidating. Maybe it's because this is the first time since I left that it's just the two of us, alone in this big house with so much pent up longing that I'm having a hard time breathing normally. I take a hefty breath and raise my eyes to him.

Tyler takes a step my way. "Finally, I have you here."

My next breath is a little shaky, perhaps due to my anxiety and uncertainty that my words come out as a question. "You have me here … for?"

He takes another step and chuckles. "Booty call?" His elated stare morphs into a serious one when I don't share the humor.

Biting on my lip, I say in a meek voice, "Please go easy on me, Tyler." Meaning, I left everything for you, and I feel a little foolish, and more than a little vulnerable.

He takes the last step to reach me and takes my hand in his. His tone turns lower and graver as he speaks next. "Why are you here?" His stare deepens. "To be with me?" He squats a bit to align our stares. A gentle, warm smile tugs at his lips as he goes on. "To be my girl? Try us out? Be my girlfriend? My woman? Either one, or all of them, pick one, whatever it takes to clear this uncertain look off your face."

I link our fingers together. "Tyler." I expel a pensive breath. "I'm just … It's overwhelming. I'm really here … with you."

He lifts our joined hands and places them on the left side of his molded chest. "Can you feel it?" he asks softly.

I nod. My own heart picks up its rhythm to Tyler's accelerated heartbeat. "I feel the same way. I nearly lost my damn mind over wanting you so much."

He leans over intending to kiss me and stops. Looking at me, he waits, I'm not sure for what.

It's one him. One me. And so much crackling, exhilarating tension. "Why aren't you kissing me?"

"I'm taking it easy on you, Kiisu. You set the pace, I'll follow."

I retrieve my hand to hug him tightly. Resting my forehead on his chest, I close my eyes. "God, I lo — " Panicked by what's almost left my mouth, my voice hitches and "L-like you," comes out somewhat croaky.

Tyler returns my hug, embracing me deeper into him. His lips touch the center of my head. There's lightness to his voice when he says to my hair, "I like you too. Incredibly much." He eases back a fraction. When I look up at him, he gives me the most adorable smile. "Tere." His dimple pops out.

"Tere." I return his smile.

"Can I kiss you now?"

Stare deep in his, I bob my head. "Please. *Everywhere*." The last word is a rasp plea.

———◆———

I'm lying on the faux fur rug, the same one I laid on a few months ago, when we began, Tyler and I, on Christmas Eve. Slowly and reverently, Tyler peels my clothes, covering my skin with succulent, hungry kisses. Till he stops.

I look up at him in confusion as I notice his sudden hesitation. He looks … pissed.

"Tyler?"

The muscle under his square jaw works overtime as he looks at me with a different kind of heat now. Heat of the angry fashion. His next words sound more like a growl. "You're wearing his damn underwear."

"It felt weird to wear Jay's pants with no underwear." I try to explain.

Tyler closes his eyes and murmurs, "I'm trying not to lose my shit."

"Tyler, what's wrong?" It's my turn to frown.

"You're wearing another man's boxers for Christ sake." Breathing in, he seems to try and collect himself. "Just take them off."

About to shimmy out of the controversial article of clothing, I do everything I can to keep the smile off my lips. "Are you … jealous?" I blink at him when realization dawns on me. "Wait a minute, oh my God, that's why you flipped all of a sudden earlier at Jay's?"

"You know how I felt coming home, looking for you and you weren't here? I thought you changed your mind. Not to mention, finding out that you chose to go to Jay first thing when you arrived…"

Humor leaves me when I look at it from his perspective, how would I have felt if I were in his shoes. "I just didn't want to be alone; I was anxious and exhausted and all I wanted was you." My eyes move between his. "No one knew when you'd be back… it felt like, at the time, that being with a friend — "

Tyler nods, still seeming a bit exasperated which, if I may, is a very sexy combo.

Needing for the tension between us to go away, I shimmy out of the nefarious fabric, sliding them aside with my toe. As I stand naked before Tyler, who's apparently quite possessive about me, I finally let my smile bloom and salute. "Mission completed, sir."

His constricted features mellow into a small, wicked, wicked grin that's followed by a breathy chuckle. And in no time, I'm back on my back with Tyler above me.

And when he kisses me again, his taste explodes in my mouth with a hint of mint, his warm breath, his addicting scent, and that perfect weight of him on me. Through our kiss, in joined forces, we get rid of his clothes.

Flesh to flesh, we halt, locking our stares, immersed in the sensation of … us. And then we lose control. Utterly and deliciously, lose control. With every breath we draw we grow more desperate. We're a chaos of burning passion. Frantic hands exploring, swollen lips seeking untouched flesh, sloppy kisses, tongue sliding against tongue, harmonized by moans and groans and a well of blasting chemistry.

My breath is stolen from me when Tyler sinks into me. I close my eyes and drop my head back, utterly consumed by the feeling of him in me, on me, in my body, in my soul. We move together, rocking against each other. Tyler seeks my mouth, grasping my bottom lip between his lips, biting it till it both stings and makes me burn for him even harder. "I can't handle myself around you," he says thrusting harder. "You have no idea how crazy you make me." With his last words and the way he moves in me I explode into blinding sensations. My body is shivering under his touch, under the feel of him. Chasing his own release, his thrusts become frenetic, fervent. With the sexiest of groans, Tyler's stills in me and lets himself go. With his weight still deliciously wrapping me in warmness and his addicting scent, he drops his head to the nook of my neck and lets his labored breath and thudding heart slow down. Wordlessly, Tyler rolls to his back, tugging me along to lie on him. And everything feels so incredibly right. So, simply right.

I doze off on Tyler's chest, weary from the long flight, from finally being with him, and from the sweet exhaustion of *being with him*.

When he stirs below me, trying to cover us with a throw blanket, I open my eyes to look at him. He smiles at me, a sweet little smile.

"You and I are … a …" I start. Tyler raises an eyebrow, waiting, his lips slightly twitched. I mirror his intimate smile. "We're a statistical anomaly. That's what we are." I state with confidence. "We. This. It never happens in real life."

Tyler grins like he and his scandalous dimple find me utterly adorable. "And yet, here we are."

"Here we are," I murmur.

He tilts his head to peck my lips. "Fucking love being a statistical anomaly with you."

CHAPTER
Five

"Some say the devil is in the details, other argue that it's God. I say, it's love. Love is in the details. You want to know how he really feels? Look for the little details. It's not just a look, a kiss, a touch, or a hug, it's the essence of these gestures. I call it the special attention signs; look carefully, if you're the one, you'll see them, you'll know."
- Told to a seventeen-year-old Ivi by her dad — an enlightening life lessons after her first heartbreak. An ordeal that lasted a whole of five hours and three minutes.

Who knew that starting the kettle could be such an elevating, joyful task. Or reaching up for a mug. Or waking up. Or breathing, for that matter. I smile to myself like a complete idiot as I drop a teabag into the white ceramic mug on the kitchen counter before me. I'm quite positive that even if I tried, I couldn't subordinate my little silly, dreamy grin. It's been plastered on my face since the moment I leisurely woke up to warm, lazy kisses along my spine that then descended from the nape of my neck down to little dimples marking the hem of my lacey boy shorts. Followed by a not so leisurely wake up. Boy did Tyler wake me up. It felt like the sheets were on fire with all the panting and burning I experienced, clutching them with my fists while my body chanted hallelujah. Making up for lost time? I support that.

Long moments after, Tyler held me in his arms as he slowly fell back asleep. Silently, I stepped out of bed, gave him another swoony glance and tiptoed to the bathroom. I can get used to waking up like this every morning. As if possible, I beam even brighter at the thought. It's almost ridiculous how I feel about this man.

I drop two slices of bread into the toaster when Adina's distinctive low, sensible heel's patter reach the kitchen. Tyler gave her the day off yesterday, making sure we had the place to ourselves. Entering the kitchen with a navy peacoat buttoned up to her neck and the warmest of smiles, Adina makes her way to me.

"I'm so, so glad you're back, darling." She wraps me in an affectionate embrace, her voice exuding geniality.

I return her hug. "I missed you, too."

We draw back with matching soft smiles. Adina unbuttons her coat with one hand, the other holds her bowler bag. "I want to hear all about Nepal." She gestures to her en suite adjacent to the kitchen. "Let me get changed first."

"I'll start the kettle," I call after her.

When Adina returns with a crisply ironed pinafore and her silver hair slicked back in a low bun, I wait for her at the long table with a mug of tea, butter honey toast and a steaming cup of coffee. Adina notices the coffee awaiting her and sends me a motherly smile. She takes the seat next to me and sips at her coffee. Attentively, she listens to me as I recount stories from my trip that right now feel like ancient history. Every so often, she nods and asks questions.

Tyler walks into the kitchen half an hour later, catching me swapping my pointer finger over a dollop of honey on my plate. He keeps watching me as I bring it to my mouth, his eyes crinkled at the corners. Praised be Jesus, the smile he has directed on me. I swallow the sweetness, hard.

"Morning," Tyler's graveled morning voice greets us.

Adina collects her empty cup and stands up. "Good morning, Tyler. Glad you made it back safely, I was worried. Last night they said on the news that they were expecting rough weather in New York."

Tyler nods, his lips tip up a little. "You never have to worry about me. Forces of nature and majeure are no match for Eli. He always makes sure I'm safe, regardless of the circumstances."

Adina's lips purse into a flat smile with a subtext that tells Tyler he should never joke about safety, or danger.

Tyler and I watch her, holding a grin at the little wordless scold she just gave Tyler. She reaches for a spray bottle and sprays the herb planter by the bay window near the sink. Turning around and noticing our subdued amusement, she shakes her head with a fond expression and leaves the room, spray bottle in hand.

Still grinning, I stretch on my tiptoes to press a light kiss on Tyler's prickly jawline. "Coffee?" I ask after he steals a kiss from my mouth, a less chaste one than the one I just gave him.

He nods, eyes eating up my sporty attire – a racerback sports top and matching, knee length capri leggings for the work out I'm planning later. Taking a seat next to Tyler, I hand him a steaming cup of coffee.

Tyler keeps his stare on me, taking a drink. My heart does a little twirl with how happy he looks as he gazes at me.

Setting the coffee on the table, Tyler's hand trails to my thigh. "Jeremy will stay over this weekend."

An affectionate smile takes over my face. "I can't wait to see him." I clear my throat. "Um, he knows I'm back, right?"

Tyler shakes his head slowly from side to side with a hint of a smile. "Thought we'd surprise him."

A little frown settles between my brows. "You sure about that? Don't you want to … prepare him?"

Tyler chuckles lightly. "He hasn't stopped talking about you since you left. There's nothing to prepare him for, he'll be thrilled."

I nod, contemplating. I raise my eyes to Tyler. "Yes, but … If he asks, well, the circumstances are a bit different now. I'm wearing another hat this time."

Tyler's subtle grin grows a little. "You shouldn't be wearing anything this time."

I twist my mouth with a little headshake. "You know what I mean."

Tyler's hand leaves my thigh to cup my cheek. "It'll be okay, Kiisu." My response stays caged in mouth as Tyler claims it with a kiss that in light speed evolves into hard fondling.

Footsteps of self-assurance followed by heel patters and an administrating throat clearing have me jerk back from Tyler's arms. In a clumsy move, I jump back to my seat, nearly losing my balance along the way. Tyler watches a tad puzzled; greater part amused. Smothering a squeal, I croak out, "Hey," moronically giving Eli a small wave. I can literally feel the apples of my cheeks warm up. Tyler's brief amused snort prompts me to send him a death threat with my glance.

"Miss Kert," Eli nods, ever the image of a pissed drill sergeant.

"Ivi," Tyler and my voice clash as we respond in stereo.

Eli nods again. "Welcome back."

"Thank you," I say, standing to adjust my disheveled clothes. The undercurrent of Eli's gaze blazing at me makes me want to hide under the table. I point my thumb in the direction of the living room, my road to salvation. "I'm going to work out."

"Before you go," Eli's commanding voice stops me in my tracks. His stare moves on to Tyler, "Will miss Kert — "

Tyler's next words interrupt whatever was about to leave Eli's mouth. "My beautiful woman's name is Ivi, and since she's here to stay, I think we can drop the formality." I give Tyler a diminutive smile. "Or Kiisu … if it works better for you."

My glare meets Tyler's smirking face, along the way catching Adina's joyous expression. I swear she looks like she's about to pull out some confetti from her apron's pocket.

Eli, seeming unfazed by Tyler's animated scolding, trades stares between Tyler and me, stopping at Tyler he asks, "Will miss Ivi join you for the award ceremony?"

Tyler turns to me as he answers Eli. "We didn't discuss it yet." Scratching his stubble coated jaw, he adds, "It's Ivi's call." He sends me a soft smile. "I'm taking it easy on her."

Feels like there are mountains of things related to Tyler's world I have no clue of. Clearing my throat, I ask, "Um, what is it? This ceremony?"

"MTV video music awards," Eli enlightens me in a stoic tone.

"It's going to be on TV?" I ask the trivial question, a bit dumbfounded by the idea. Tyler's stardom, public persona, is not something I took into account when weighing my decision to come back. Or perhaps I just kept it hidden at the back of my mind, disinclined to give it too much thought. Maybe I just knew that it would simply freak me out and make me take a few too many steps back.

"Yes. The TV part stands for television, miss Kert." Eli deadpans.

Surprised by Tyler's snap as he says Eli's name admonishingly, I bite on my lip, feeling more than a little uncomfortable. It all happened so fast, but it's clear to everyone in the room that Tyler has lost his patience.

Tyler brings his coffee to his lips, listening to Eli who quickly changes the narrative as he starts filling Tyler in on something that has to do with some benefit event or something like that. Tyler's eyes move to me, slowly drinking me in, head to toe, as I'm about to excuse myself once more. He sets the mug on the table. "I don't know," Tyler tells Eli while standing up and walking over to where I stand. "That venue," he says on a breath, dropping to sit on his haunches before me. Startled, both Eli's, Adina and my gaze follow him to where he's crouched by my feet. "There's something about it," he says, signaling for me to bring my foot up to his thigh. "I don't like it. See if they can find an alternative."

Finishing my shoe lace tie, he gently removes my foot back to the floor. My heart climbs up to lodge somewhere in my throat. I look at him in sweet bewilderment. *Love is in the details.* Slowly standing up, Tyler kisses my cheek and turns to Eli who's watching Tyler with his mouth slightly hanging. Squinting my gaze, I catch Adina nodding to herself with that clandestine smile she's developed since seeing Tyler and I kiss after Christmas.

Tyler's hand moves to cup my neck. He leans forward, "We'll talk about the awards thing later, when we're alone." Dipping lower, he gently kisses my lips.

Eyes slightly cast down with emotions, I mumble, "Later," before leaving the kitchen.

CHAPTER
Six
CHAPTER

Diet Journal, Day 1: Weight loss goal: 10 pounds. Time to complete goal: 2 days. Summary: Not happening, dude! I don't do diet! ...and what am I going to wear!?

Ivi's I'm – freaking – out – I'm – going – to – mingle – with – beautiful – famous – national – treasures – journal entry less than a week before the award ceremony.

"Who's going to be there?" I ask Tyler, admiring the familiar backdrop we pass on our ride to meet with some people at Raging Bitch, that tiny, charming dive bar Jay once took me to. I couldn't stop my elated snort when Tyler told me how the bar got its glamorous name. Apparently, a long while ago, the bar was called Kirk's after its owner, but after his divorce a few years back, Kirk decided to name it in honor of his ex.

Taking a turn, eyes on the road ahead, Tyler answers my question, "Killer, Max, Jay. I think Killer is brining Sophia."

I nod to the window.

"So, did you decide what you want to do?"

I give Tyler a quizzical side glance.

"The VMAs." Tyler elaborates, bringing back the MTV award ceremony we discussed before leaving home. Home ... Jury's still out on this one. To me, it feels like we're taking giant steps, Tyler and I, even though we've agreed to take-us-slowly. I should really bring up the thing that I've been trying to discuss with Tyler, but couldn't find the appropriate time. Or simply chickened out.

I worry my lips, turning to look at him. "Do you mind waiting to out me?"

Tyler twists his mouth, taking a pensive pause. He shakes his head. "No," comes out on an exhale. "I'm okay with whatever makes you feel comfortable." Pulling the car to a stop in the bar's parking lot, Tyler pivots to face me. "Like we agreed, you set the pace." Then, "Fame, no matter how you get it is a trap. I don't want you sucked into it before you're completely prepared."

I take his hand in mine and bring it to my lips for a light kiss. Linking our fingers together, I look up at him. "I just feel like we need some time alone together, with nothing influencing us. I think that for now I want to be selfish, have our thing to ourselves. I'm well-aware of the fact that I'm sharing you with the world, but sharing what we have … it's too soon for me."

Tyler nods, wordlessly supporting me.

"Umm, speaking of us," I give Tyler a quick, hesitant smile. "I was thinking about finding my own place." Assessing, I study his features as they set in a displeased, quizzical expression.

Tyler folds his arms across his chest. "Where's that coming from?"

"We're … how shall I put it? We've just started, um…dating, and—" I try to put into words thoughts I've been struggling to puzzle up in my own head since I boarded the plane back to L.A.

Seeming to evaluate what I'm trying to get across, Tyler intercepts my attempt at reasoning. "Ivi, Ivi. Look at me." Getting my attention, he goes on. "We're way past *dating*." Dating comes out with a fairly derisive lilt. "For the life of me, I can't see any logical reason for you to find your own place. I have over eight bedrooms, not that I want you in any other bedroom but mine."

A loud thump on the driver's window has us both jerk to face it. Max's toothy grin glued to the window, fogging it up, prompts collective easy chuckles from Tyler and me.

"Dimwit," Tyler murmurs under his breath. Rolling down the window just enough for Max to hear him, Tyler says, "We're coming," and he rolls it back up. He turns back to me. "Whatever is going on in that pretty head of yours, stop it. We're together, and we are everything that it stands for."

Reassuring as his words are, there's still this feeling, this niggling feeling that maybe we're putting the cart before the wild horse that is our unusual coupling.

I clear my throat. Returning Tyler's calculating stare from under my lashes, I clear my throat again. "By thinking about finding my own place," I bite my lip. "I mean, I sort of found one." I choose not to add that it's in one of the worst neighborhoods in the area, nor that it smells of the Indian food from the restaurant on the first floor, or the suspicious dark crimson spot I found next to the fold up bed.

Tyler's frown deepens. He parts his lips to speak, but before he's able to utter a word, I shake my head and say, "Tyler, please let me do this my way."

———— ◆ ————

"What up people?" Killer greets us as we join the gang sitting around two high tables joined together. Max, Jay, Killer, Sophia and a new face that belongs to a guy called Zade.

I smile at the group and Tyler nods. "Everything's copacetic," he throws his phone and wallet on the table.

"My love," Max exclaims and rises to stand, his palm spread on his heart. Heading our way, he manages to squeeze himself between Sophia who remains with her arms spread, ready for a hug, and me.

I squeal when Max's arms band around me and lift me up. "Put your lips on mine, Lady Ivi."

Wordless, but with a look that could easily slaughter a grownup human being, Tyler releases me from Max's roaming hands. He tugs me on to his side, giving Max another warning glance.

Pocketing his hand into his leather pants, Max shakes his head and tips his chin at Tyler. "What does he have that I don't?"

Tyler rolls his eyes while I let out a giggle.

With a sweet little smile, I look up at Tyler. "My heart."

I guess "my heart" is some sort of passcode for: "Tyler please stick your tongue in my mouth and suck the life out of me by the mother of all kisses." Because that's what he does, catching me utterly off guard. Stunned and with my knees somewhat weak, I gasp a little to bring myself back to breathing human form rather than a frothing, panting putty in Tyler Lee Adams' hands.

Mustering nonchalance which I'm pretty sure no one buys, what with the heat my cheeks are radiating, I face the group. The group of smirking faces, that is. I squint at Tyler, ready to shoot him a scolding glance. I'm mildly baffled by his cool demeanor. Feels like he's more than a few steps ahead in this game. I'm still getting used to being with him, especially in company of other people while he seems to have zero damns to give.

Not more than five minutes later, I feel at home. Like I've never left. The group is entirely indifferent about me being with Tyler, as though it was anticipated. Each with a drink and a smile, conversation flows with random laughter, chatter, and quiet pauses as sips are stolen from glasses and bottles. In the middle of recounting an anecdote of that one-time Tyler fell asleep sitting straight up with coconut water in his hand in his dressing room during the last tour, Killer's eyes drop to Max's pants.

"What up with the Village People look, man?" Killer asks Max.

Our collective attention turns to Max's tight, as in I'm not sure how he'll manage to peel them off later, leather pants.

Max grins. "Besides looking like a god?" That earns him a couple of eye rolls, a snort, and a peanut to his forehead. "See it's actually genius." He slaps his leather clad thigh. "If I get shitfaced and piss myself no one will notice."

Tyler's animated gaze meets mine and he shakes his head. He leans closer and whispers, "He really shouldn't be let out on his own, let alone be allowed to mingle with other people." I respond with a grin.

"How does your mind even go there," Jay says in mocked bewilderment and adds, "it's beyond disturbing." Low laughter follows.

Leaning a little closer, Tyler's lips press against the pulsating vein in my neck. "I'm so glad you're here," he murmurs to my slowly heating skin.

Catching Sophia's eyes on us, I reciprocate Tyler's kiss with a chaste peck on his cheek, bringing to an end our little display of affection. I'm not one to shy away from a little PDA, but when the audience is this attentive, it makes me a tad uncomfortable. In an attempt to avoid Sophia's laser eyes, my own gaze roams around the room only to find out that we, our group, are the only patrons in the bar. "Slow night tonight," I say as an afterthought.

"Kirk closes up the place for us," Tyler says casually.

I frown. "Doesn't it hurt his business?"

Tyler gives me a gentle smile that comes together with a tender gaze. "Don't worry. I make sure he's compensated for that."

"You do?" The notion surprises me. My heart sighs with warmth. "That's kind of you."

Tyler's lips tug at the side. He shrugs. "I try."

I look at him. Really look at him. My eyes bore into his, and I can't take them away. The small things he does. The real man. His kindness, his sweetness. I choke up on feelings. He cocks his head, eyes running between mine. The way he looks at me, the way I see myself through his eyes. I've never felt as special. I run my gaze between his eyes. My adoration transpires though the warm smile easing my lips.

"What?" He asks through a sweet chuckle.

I shrug. "Just you." And then I add, "Being you."

Tyler's arm winds around my shoulder, squeezing me to him. He plants a kiss to my temple, taking a lungful. On an exhale, he whispers, "I adore you, Kiisu."

Tonight, feeling ridiculously happy, I let go a little, letting myself drink a bit more than my usual one glass limit. Sipping from my second appletini, I raise my eyes to Sophia who takes the seat next to me, the one Jay just vacated. Sophia takes a swig of her own drink and rolls her eyes at the conversation about vintage guitars taking place around us. "I need some girl talk, like right now."

I clink my glass with hers, "Talk to me." I let her pull me into a conversation about my return, one that involves more questions than I'm inclined to answer, but I go with it. Alcohol does that to me, makes me friendly and chatty.

———— ◆ ————

"Now?" I ask Tyler, giving him a sidelong glance. He trades glances between the window shield and me, seeming determined. "It's what? Midnight?"

"So?" He retorts. "You said you found a place, I want to see it."

"Do we really need to do it right now?" Sure, instead of going home to the warm bed awaiting us, why don't we roam the streets instead.

"Yeah."

When no other reaction besides the resolute one word comes from his side, I shake my head in reluctant compliance. "Fine." I give him the address.

Tyler is quiet throughout the longish ride, besides one little comment about how far away my "new place" is from his house. I don't respond to his comment. Seems like mentioning that I can't afford anything near him would start a whole new conversation I'm not too keen on having.

"This is the place?" Tyler asks twenty minutes later, narrowing his gaze under the sole lamppost in the relatively dark street. When a group of young men pass by us, Tyler's lips flatten into a grim line. I squint at the group with their beer cans in hand and their overall juvenile delinquent appearance.

"Ivi — "

Just by his tone alone, I know what's coming next, and quickly intercept his next words. "Tyler," I take his hand in mine. "Let me do it my way." My soft smile doesn't do much to appease him.

"Christ, Ivi." His expression hardens. "You'll get yourself — "

Once again, I cut him off. "Tyler, I can take care of myself. This place has nothing on some of the places I've been before."

"And this should reassure me somehow?" Tyler's eyes shine with exasperation. "Do you even know how important you are to me?"

I love you so much, sits on the tip of my tongue. "You're important to me too, Tyler. Immensely," comes out of my mouth instead.

"Am I?" His eyes narrow at me. "Then don't put yourself at risk, don't do it for my sake."

"You're not playing fair."

"I'm not?" He folds his arms across his chest. "Caring about you and trying to prevent you from getting assul ... Jesus, I don't even want to think about it."

Seeing that this impasse we found ourselves in won't resolve itself, I try a different approach. "Umm, how about I ask Ben to check the locks on the door just before I move in?"

Tyler throws his eyes up, saying: as if that'll help. "The only way I'll be okay with this, which I still don't understand why you insist on it, is have him assign someone to you."

"A bodyguard?" I swear, I really try to stop the snort that follows, which only makes Tyler look a little less jubilant. "Listen, we're not getting anywhere, why don't we just drop it. I promise to be careful." Flushing a smile at him, I add, "I'll get pepper spray!"

Tyler's testy expression deepens. "When are you planning to move out?"

Forgive me for beautifying the truth. At this moment, I'm pretty positive that if I uttered the original date, *tomorrow*, I'll start world war three. "Ah, sometime toward the end of next week."

Giving me an inscrutable glance, he turns to look out the window. "I'm asking you not to, that's my final comment." He ends our talk, bringing the engine to life.

It's only when we get home and get ready for bed that Tyler appears to finally calm down … a little. Not sure if our earlier disagreement constitutes a fight, an argument perhaps, but whatever it was, it weighs like lead in my stomach.

We lie silently in bed, Tyler though somewhat less irritated is still distant, making me second guess my decision to move out. Maybe if it's that important to him that I stay, I should just stay. Stay. I slowly scoot closer to him, glad to find his arm open, inviting me to snuggle by his side.

An incoming text ping sounds like a horn as it rips the silence in the room.

With his free hand, Tyler retrieves his phone from the nightstand. I can feel him shake his head before letting out a frustrated huff.

"What's wrong?" I ask in a small voice.

"It's Eli," he says and flings the device back to its resting place. "There are already speculations about you."

What? How? "Me?" I croak out.

"Someone must have talked." Tyler turns to lie on his side, his eyes searching mine under the dimly lit room. "Welcome to my world."

I don't answer, I just lean forward to kiss his lips. Faking coolness, I show him with my kisses and body how nothing but him really matters.

CHAPTER
Seven

CHAPTER

"Love is simple and pure, we are the ones who complicate it with our doubts and insecurities and the fear of giving ourselves completely to someone else."
A philosophical thought penetrating Ivi's mind as she stretches before a run.

I tie my shoelaces and secure my phone in the armband wrapped around my bicep, ready to go for a run. The sun painting the day in bright warmth lured me to have my run outside, in the open fresh air rather than in the confines of the indoor gym. I pop by the kitchen to refill my water bottle, finding Adina setting up a tray with morning goodies.

"Morning." I steal a fresh strawberry from the tray. "Are they in the living room?" I ask Adina, referring to a meeting between Tyler, Eli, and the guys Tyler mentioned while kissing my neck just before he left the bedroom half an hour ago.

"Yes, darling," Adina nods to the pot of steaming coffee.

Snatching another piece of fruit and a nice bundle of cookies, I wink at her. "I'll use the backdoor, don't want to interfere with matters of great importance."

Adina mirrors my cheeky grin.

Passing by Oscar, the guard manning the main gate, I offer a quick good morning and the bundle of cookies I "borrowed" from the tray. He grins at me in return and presses the button that lifts the gate. This place is secured like a military base. Plunging my earbuds in, I bring up the music app. Taking a lungful of the crisp, late morning air, I commence my stretching. Short moments later, I wave at Oscar and start my run. It's a beautiful morning of bright sun and green leafy trees dancing in the light wind. With a thin smile on my face I head up the small hill that leads to the main road surrounded by lofty palm trees.

As I jog to The Dunwells singing in my ears about love and communication, a movement in my periphery has me glance sideways. A lean brunette jogging by sends me a runners'camaraderie grin and a nod. I reciprocate with a quick smile. As I continue my run, pushing myself a little harder, I notice her matching my pace, running beside me. She pulls out one of her EarPods, keeping our synched rhythm. I do the same, tilting my head in question.

"You live around here?" she asks through labored breath.

Not giving too much thought to her question, I nod, throwing my thumb back. "Up the hill."

"Oh, in the big mansion?" she asks, still lightly smiling.

"Yeah," I return absentmindedly. Friendly people in this neighborhood.

"What's your name?" she asks next.

"Ivi."

She slows her run to face me. I do the same, a bit puzzled by her overly friendly ways.

"Ivi." She sends me a sweet smile that in a blink of an eye turns fairly malicious. And before I know it, her rounded fist lands smack-dab on my left eye. "Tyler belongs to Brooklyn, you little bitch." And before I'm able to comprehend the last few seconds she sprints away.

My hand flies to my throbbing eye as I watch her disappear around the corner. Gape-mouthed, I stay frozen in my place for some long shocking moments. The pain radiating from my upper cheekbone and the idea that someone assaulted me leave me utterly flabbergasted. Confused, somewhat humiliated and harboring a smarting pain, I turn back. I jog lightly, tilting my head sideways as I reach the main gate. Oscar raises his hand. Teasing, he asks me if I'm out of shape. Making sure to conceal my injured eye, I fabricate a smile and give him a lame excuse about preferring the air-conditioned gym.

I'm too startled to comprehend that I just entered the house from the main door, realizing I'm at the living room's threshold a second too late. The last thing I want right now is to have everyone's attention on me. Ducking my face, I rapidly walk by the guys, throwing a quick "hi," hoping that my state wasn't transpired through the short word.

"Ivi?" It's Tyler's voice that stops me from taking the last few steps out of the room.

"Mmm," I answer with my back to the group.

"All okay?" There's a touch of concern to Tyler's question.

I nod. The cadence of Tyler's voice is a trigger for my eyes to fill up with a misty screen. "Yeah," floats out of my mouth. "I'm ok — ay." My last word comes out broken as I feel Tyler's hands clutch around my shoulders.

"Kiisu?" Tyler says softly only for me to hear, gently turning me to look at him. Noticing my shinning eyes, he stoops to align our stares and it's then that he notices the pink, puffed skin around my eye. Concern hardens his features, it must look just like it feels. "What happened?" he gently touches my skin, I flinch at the contact. "Who did this to you?"

And that's as long as I can hold it all in. My lips quiver with the first tear that rolls out of my eye. Tyler's arm bounds around me, holding me tight to his chest. With an accelerating heartbeat, Tyler says in a voice that carries no pleasantry, "Everyone out."

"She okay?" comes a response from the group. "Mary P. what's wrong?" It's Max this time.

I feel Tyler looking at them over his shoulder. "Show's over. Eli, I swear, get everyone the fuck out of here. Now!"

An immediate hustle of hushed voices and foot shuffling comes next. Someone clears his voice, "Tyler, what's going on?" It's Eli.

"Let's sit down. Come, Kiis," Arms secured around me, Tyler leads me to take a seat on the sofa.

I lift my face, to a certain degree embarrassed and very much confused, to look at Tyler and then turn to Eli. Eli's brows furrow, his jaw sets in a tense line.

"Tell us what happened," Tyler's comforting embrace and soft voice cajoles.

I cover my face with both hands and huff, dropping my hands to my thighs, I shrug. "I'm not sure." Both men regard me intently. "I went for a run and this woman appeared out of nowhere and joined me."

Tyler's eyes run over my face. Eli nods.

"Adina, can you bring us an icepack, please?" Tyler calls out, his fingers caressing down my arms. "Sorry, go on," he says to me.

"She seemed friendly and asked where I lived. Then she asked for my name and before I knew it, she confronted me about …" I turn to look at Tyler. "You belonging to Brooklyn and that I should stay away."

Anger washes over Tyler's face like a wild wave of fire. He throws Eli a look, which Eli counters with some sort of agreement. Tyler's hand comes up to cover his mouth, his muscle distinctively sawing under his jaw. "Get Ben," he utters curtly.

"Here's the icepack," Adina enters the room. When she sees me, her eyes round, "what happened to you?"

I shake my head, opting to communicate: nothing serious. I attempt to send her a thin smile.

Tyler extends his hand for the icepack. He nods at Adina, and turns to me, gently pressing the cold package against my smarting, sensitive skin. "Does it hurt?" he asks, his eyes trailing over my face.

I nod. "It burns." I reach my hand to take the icepack from him, but he doesn't let go.

Adina and Eli watch us as Tyler regards me pensively. He turns to Eli, "We'll be in my room. Cancel whatever we had for today."

"Tyler, there's no need for that — " I try to interject.

Tyler just shakes his head at me. "Get Ben to have someone assigned to Ivi today!"

"Of course," Eli affirms.

Wordlessly, Tyler stands, offering me his hand. When I'm on my feet, he secures my hand in his. "There's this rental contract Ivi signed, have that cancelled. Sort it out, if needed, compensate them for breaching the contract at the last minute."

"Sure thing. Anything else?" Eli responds.

"No."

"Tyler, should I bring anything up?" Adina asks as Tyler starts walking us toward the stairs.

At this point I just rest my head on his shoulder, letting him take care of me.

"Kiisu? Some cold water maybe."

"That would be great, thanks."

———— ◆ ————

"I'm sorry you went through this because of me," Tyler says as he runs a foamy sponge down my arm, cradling me to his chest in the warm, comforting bath.

"It's not your fault, you can't really control crazy people." I turn a little to kiss his prickled jaw. "Well, apparently I've sinned the greatest sin of all, I fell for their God," I say in a scornful tone.

I can feel Tyler cringe behind me. "I'm no one's anything. I'm Jeremy's dad. And I'm your … yours."

I turn to face him, splashing some water and bubbles over the rim of the bath as I straddle him. I give him a thin smile. "I'll take a punch any day for you to be mine."

Tyler's lips arch into a sweet smile, calling for his dimple to join. "I'm so gone for you, Kiisu."

We sit in silence for some pensive moments, each in our own bubble of contemplation.

I clear my throat, "Umm, Tyler?"

"Yeah." Tyler's arms draw soft trails over my exposed skin, up from my navel to the valley of my breasts and back.

"I won't be moving out." I take a pause, slightly craning my neck to look at him. I've thoroughly dissected this — living together for some good intense months, me taking care of his child, being a part of his family and friends in a sense sped our getting to know each other to levels of intimacy a year of dating wouldn't even begin to scratch. Yet, there are still things to be said, clarified. By the look in his eyes, the diminutive twitches of his features or the cadence of his voice alone I can decipher Tyler's mood. "But for future reference, please don't dismiss me. Don't take the liberty of overruling my decisions. I can understand where it came from, a place of protection, of wanting to keep me safe." I let out an exhale. "For us to work, I need to be my own person. You need to respect my decisions, just like I do yours."

Tyler's arms band around my waist. "I will. There's nothing I want more than for us to work."

"We're equals in this relationship, Tyler."

His voice is low, almost a whisper as he says, "No, we are not. You have the upper hand, Kiisu. There's nothing I wouldn't do for you."

Eight

"Meet me there, where the stars turn silver. This time I promise
I'll bare my soul. This time I promise, I'll never let you go."
Never Again, *Tyler Lee Adams new single.*

"**G**od, you're…" I roll to my back still catching my breath. I turn my head, cheek pressed against the pillow and drink Tyler in. He mimics me, turning to his side. His tan skin now harboring a light blush, his breath labored, his eyes molten brown, boring into mine. "You're killing me," I say on a whisper. "In the best of ways."

Tyler's lip lifts at the corner into a half, sinful smile. He reaches his hand to brush a lock of hair clung to my cheek. "What can I say, every god damn thing about you turns me on."

I lick my tender lips, giving him a soft smile. Tyler scoots closer to bring his lips to mine.

"You fucking sneeze and I find it incredibly sexy," he says to my parted lips with his rough morning voice.

My giggle funnels into his mouth as he kisses me through a smile. "You're adorably cray cray."

Untangling myself from the addiction that is Tyler's embrace, I drop my legs off the bed. Turning to look at Tyler over my shoulder, I ask, "So you're not going to tell me who's your plus one tonight?"

A wicked glee adorns his eyes as he shakes his head. "Nope." He sends me a teasing grin. "You lost your right to ask me that when you refused to be my date." I know he's just joking, and he's absolutely okay with me not being ready to be outed as Tyler Lee Adams' girlfriend at such a covered event. There are more than enough speculations as it is. I'm not in a hurry to officially put it out there. But the fact that he won't tell me who is going to be his date for the music awards tonight irritates more than a little. "C'mere." He sends his arm to my waist.

Before he's able to reach me, I jump off the bed. "Nah ah, there won't be any c'meres for you now." I walk over to the bathroom and just before closing the door behind me, turn to give him a cheeky stare. "Hey Tyler, …" Tyler lifts his brows in question. I bring both hands toward my nose and feign a loud sneeze. Tyler's laughter follows me as I close the door behind me.

———◆———

Inwardly laughing to myself, I listen to Zara as she goes on in light speed tempo about her plan for me for today. I rest my hands on the back of a nearby chair, grasping for something solid, , feeling like I need to hold on or I'll be swept away by the torrential outpouring of words . I raise my stare to wordlessly ask Tyler to rescue me. Tyler grins at me and mouths "told you," before giving me a small wave and leaving through the front door.

"C'mon there's no one I can't handle, I'm sure you're exaggerating," I told Tyler earlier when he warned me that his stylist, Zara, could be a handful. Nope, he wasn't exaggerating. Zara is indeed, as Tyler said, a petite tornado. In the last ten minutes since we've been introduced, I've already learned about her dog of an ex-husband. Her love for "good ole' Scotch" and "good 'ole macho men". How she thinks I have angelic facial features. How I have a fitted figure that a pound less would be perfect. Healthy, yet boring hair. And that her period can be declared a new form of torture. I keep blinking at her in stunned silence as she confirms a list of things we should get done before tonight. I lost her somewhere after putting my foot down and refusing to get a colon hydrotherapy. I don't really care about having a little puffed tummy as she puts it, no tube is getting anywhere near my heiny, thank you very much.

"So, are we ready?" she finally asks.

I nod, seriously considering running out the door screaming.

More than twenty minutes later, where I'm slouched on a heated recliner, my feet wrapped up in aromatic seaweed mask, while I'm sipping the most delicious tea, I realize that, after all, Zara is an angel and we could definitely become best friends.

Zara, firing styling advice my way, flips through a tablet, showing me different styles of dresses for tonight. "I think we're fine," she says not long after. "I like your style, but I think that maybe for tonight you'd want to go with something a bit more ..." She raises both hands dramatically. "Make a statement! You'll get lost in the crowd if we go with something uninspiring."

"You know I'm not going as Tyler's date, right?" I try to make a valid point to tone down her need for a grandeur effect.

She pats my hand with a lenient smile. "That doesn't mean you can't shine, babe."

Well, who can argue with that? I let Zara take the reins from here.

By the time we get home, about an hour and a half before we should leave for the evening, I am a proud new owner of six gorgeous evening gowns, and a dozen exquisite pairs of shoes. Not to mention, I'm waxed, pampered and beautified like I've never been before. Seriously though, my skin never glowed like it does right now as I observe myself in the mirror with fascination.

"I think you should wear the red one," Zara tips her chin at the collection of dresses now hanging in my half of Tyler's dressing room. The red one is one of the dresses Zara chose for me, one of the "unique" ones that will push me outside my comfort zone and make me look like a goddess, her words not mine.

I'm still a bit hesitant with that one, what with the way it clings to my skin and the tiny amount of skin left unexposed. The sound of my cell indicating an incoming text has me shrugging in agreement before picking up the phone.

Tyler: Surviving?

Hardly. You know, it's tough being the center of a pampering crusade.

Tyler: Glad to hear they are taking good care of my woman.

No, it's not pathetic at all how my body reacts to that little sentence. I never knew I could physically swoon. A tiny wicked smile blooms on my lips as I send him a response. An image of a sphynx cat with the following caption:

This little kitty and your Kiisu have something in common now.

The little dots on my phone jump as Tyler types his reply.

Tyler: What do you have in common with the coatless puss?

Not a second passes before the next message lands in my phone.

Tyler: You just killed me woman.

My hair is being styled into a sexy updo, and the makeup artist practically goes to town on my face with an evening look concept. I never had that much make up on my face at once. I feel like I'm playing dress-up in the remaining time till the guys come back home and we're ready to go.

"And it's a wrap!" Zara declares with utter enthusiasm as the makeup artist adds the last touch of glimmer to my deep, deep cleavage.

"Oh wow," expels out of my lips as I stand before the mirror. I look dazzling in a very provocative kind of way. For a moment there, I remind myself of a sexy Bratz doll with the heavy makeup and the tight, sensuous red number I'm wearing. I look glamorous, I have to give it to Zara, but even if you look really carefully there's nothing of the real me in the glitzy reflection looking back at me via the mirror.

"The guys are downstairs waiting for you," Zara says, urging me to leave the mirror and go downstairs.

My steps as I take the stairs are somewhat hesitant and they have nothing to do with the high heels I'm wearing. My heart pounds in my chest as I take the last few steps, meeting Tyler's gaze. Tyler's lips part as he scans me head to toe. His brows slightly bunch before his lips arch in a predatory smile. I fidget as Tyler walks over to me, offering me his hand.

"Young Ivi, wow," Jay says, from his place beside Tyler. "You don't look so young and innocent anymore."

Exactly, Jay.

Tyler leans in to press a soft kiss to my cheek. Easing off, he parts his lips, about to speak.

"Tyler?" Jeremy, in a tux and jeans, stops in his tracks with a chocolate bar in his hand. "Oh hi," his eyes drop to Tyler's and my joined hands and up again to look at me. He cocks his head, looking at me as if he knows me from somewhere. "I-Ivi?"

I let go of Tyler's hand and rush to wrap Jeremy in my arms. "Missed me?" I say over a watery smile. God, I missed this adorable kid so freaking much.

Jeremy's toothy smile shines at me, "You're back."

"Couldn't stay away from you." Our mutual smiles grow.

"Are you, ah, staying?" He asks, his stare moves on to Tyler for confirmation.

Tyler nods with a smile I'm having a hard time to decode.

"Sweet!"

Tyler takes a few steps to reach us. Wrapping his hand around Jeremy's shoulder, he grins at me. "How do you like my plus one?"

I watch them both, taken aback by how similar they look now. With the same outfit and the same buzzed hairstyle Jeremy is a spitting image of his dad. My chest fills with warmness and adoration, I can hardly breath. "It's perfect."

They both grin at me with that heart melting smile of theirs.

Eyeing me awkwardly, Jeremy twist his mouth. "The other day, um, I read in one of those women magazines they have in waiting rooms that makeup contains lead, and you know, it can cause allergies and it can sometimes affect the nervous system."

I let out an uncomfortable sigh-laugh. Seeing Jeremy made me forget my look and how I feel about it. Feeling like a stranger in my own body never felt so real.

"We should get going," Eli's commanding voice comes from the vicinity of the kitchen, followed by his distinctive footfall.

Sensing my unease Tyler turns to face me. "You okay?"

I fidget some more. Taking a hefty breath, I look at him from under my lashes. "Um, yeah. Yeah, sure. Of course."

Tyler tilts his head, looking at me as though he is not buying what I'm selling.

I exhale. "It's just, I'm not trying to be ungrateful, but, well — " I fidget again. "I feel a little strange with all of this," I gesture with my hand over myself. "I just, I — I really don't feel like myself."

Tyler listens to me attentively till Eli calls him, motioning to his watch. Tyler shakes his head at Eli who doesn't look so pleased.

"Ivi, listen to me, if it doesn't work for you, go put on something you feel comfortable wearing. Never change. Not for me, not for anyone, you're so perfect just the way you are. I'd never want you to feel out of place or uncomfortable for my sake."

"You're sure?" I look up at him. "We don't have time, do we?"

Tyler ducks to give me a chaste kiss. "Go, we'll wait for you here."

Avoiding Eli's not so sympathetic stare, I kick off my heels, bend to grab them and hurry up the stairs. Jeremy, calling my name, stops me from taking the last two stairs leading to the third floor.

Bending over the banister, I call, "What?"

"You missed your room."

Oh. My eyes dart to Tyler's.

"Ivi is staying in my room," Tyler clarifies.

Jeremy's head jerks back in surprise. His eyes, from behind the blue frame of his glasses look my way, then to Tyler. "Where are *you* staying then?"

Tyler points his finger up. "In my room."

Jeremy does the looking at us thing again. His lips part a little. "Are you guys?" Another gaze bounces between Tyler and me. "Eww gross," Jeremy says next, pretending to gag by shoving his finger into his mouth.

Nothing can stop my blush. Tyler chuckles. "Ivi's my girlfriend."

Jeremy pretends to retch again, then throws Tyler a mischievous grin. "Then, well played, old man." A brighter smile light up his face as he looks up my way. "So that means you're staying for good, right?"

I smile back and make myself scarce, letting Tyler deal with the "for good" part.

Less than ten minutes later, with my hair hanging loose over my back, half of the makeup I had before and a satin black dress with an exposed back that reaches just shy of my knees, I make my way back to the guys.

Tyler is talking to Jay who has his back to the stairs as I take the last steps. Noticing me, Tyler stops talking and gapes at me. He brings his hand to his heart and mouths, "Wow."

Light warmness covers my cheeks.

"What you looking at, Boo-Boo?" Jay asks mid-turn.

"My future," Tyler's voice reaches me low and raspy, tugging at my inside in the best possible way. Eyes locked with mine, he walks over to me.

"Oh, now you look like yourself! Much better," Jeremy says over a grin.

Reaching me, Tyler sends his arms to my waist. Looking at me for a still moment, he bends, his lips nearing my ear. "So incredibly beautiful. Nothing looks better on you than you."

CHAPTER
Nine

CHAPTER

"No talking to the stars, no interacting with them. Don't act out, don't draw
attention. Don't do anything that makes you stand out to the camera."
Seat-fillers and non-celebrity guest rules handed to Ivi by one of the
ushers at the VMAs.

I get giddier as our limo driver veers the car into the queue of glitzy cars waiting to pour out VIPs into the parted sea of eager fans and no less eager photographers waiting by the red carpet. Not having Tyler next to me doesn't help my pent-up anxiety. It's not every day that a small-town girl gets to rub elbows with celebrities of greater existence, or be at such a glamorous event for that matter. I'm well aware that if Tyler were by my side it would have greatly diminished my apprehension, but it was my choice to not do that. My choice not to expose us to the world in such a public, heavily covered event.

"Hey," Jay's voice infiltrates my growing bubble of concern. "It'll be fun, you'll see." I give him half a smile. "I know I'm no Tyler Lee Adams," he says with an amused lilt, "but I'm here for you." He winks.

I squeeze his hand, "You're the bestest."

Not long after, I feel like I've been swept into a parallel universe, standing with a glass of champagne in the grand foyer, absorbing the past twenty minutes or so. Luckily, the crowd gathered around the entrance to the building has realized we're "no ones" and has concentrated their attention elsewhere. However, the entire experience was, to put it simply, overwhelming. It's all so … glamorous and different. The attendees certainly brought their A-game in outstanding ensembles. Looking at them from the side, I have to admit, they do look like a superior breed. I now understand Zara's insistence of me wearing something unique.

I smile thinking about the fan's reaction to Tyler as he walked in with Jeremy. Jeremy literally shined and that look he gave Tyler as they stepped on the red carpet expanded my heart to impossible proportions. So much admiration in those witty brown eyes. I hope someone had captured it for Tyler to see. I need to get my hands on that photo if it does exist out there.

"Your boyfriend is coming for you," Jay tells me, tipping his chin toward Tyler and Jeremy walking our way.

My eyes get stuck on Tyler, keenly drinking him in. The way he moves, the aura surrounding him, so easily taking the attention of the room. With a custom fitted white button down, the tux embracing his wide figure and the bowtie with stylish contrast to the distressed jeans and worn army boots, he's a sinful, erotic dream personified. I can't take my eyes off him. Closing the distance between us, Tyler's attention is homed in on me, looking like he's about to haul me over his shoulder. A look of lust. A look of possession. A notion that just adds to my pulsing heart and the currents of thrill cruising through me.

A photographer urging Tyler to look his way sobers me up. For a moment there I forgot where we are. A place where I'd like to keep Tyler and me under wraps. Tyler nods at him, wraps his arm around a grinning Jeremy, letting the photographer take the sought for shot.

"Enjoying yourself, Kiisu?" Tyler asks moments later, standing by my side.

"Yeah, I am." I try to shake off the dreamy glimmer my eyes take when I look at him.

Tyler gives me a soft smile, his voice lower as he tilts his head my way, "I can't even handle how beautiful you look. Can't wait to get home and have you all for myself."

My lips tip up as I return his heated gaze. "Then hurry up with your being a star thing and take me home, Tyler."

"Being a celebrity is exhausting!" Both Tyler's and my eyes dart to Jeremy. Jay grins at him, as Jeremy huffs. "Having your photos taken all the time, and all these people wanting a piece of you." He massages his jaw. "All this smiling. Jeez." Jeremy tugs at his bowtie and shakes his head. "Exhausting!"

"Well, good thing it'll all be over in an hour, ah bud?" Tyler says. "Ben will take you home soon."

I add, "Maybe start with small doses, don't wear yourself out."

Jeremy frowns, his glasses sitting a bit crooked on the bridge of his nose. "But — "

"School night," Tyler says over a grin. "And anyhow, we don't want your stardom to exhaust you, do we?"

I move over to adjust the kid's glasses on his nose. "Leaving early will just make you more mysterious, will keep 'em wanting more."

Tyler and Jay chuckle when Jeremy rolls his eyes at me.

"I need to get ready." Tyler throws back the rest of his drink, depositing the empty glass on one of the high tables peppering the place. "Jer, I'll talk to you tomorrow."

Jeremy nods.

Tyler turns to Jay, "Take care of my woman for me, cuddle bug."

Saluting, Jay grins. "Aye aye, smitten kitty."

A bustle of people taking their places lasts until the lights blink, signaling for the last attendees to find their seats before the ceremony begins. With Tyler being one of the most famous singers in the house tonight, his guests' seats, aka, us — his entourage, are in the best location. Right in the middle of the first row behind the bulk of celerity seats.

Jeremy is beside himself with excitement every time some other famous being takes a seat near us. It's kind of funny to see how Jeremy is starting to take notice of the opposite sex, to watch him blush and get all flustered, and goofy when another deep cleavage walks by. Deep, round and healthy, those can be found in abundance. He looks like one of those silly cartoons with their eyes popping out of their heads.

After a long silence, the curtains roll up, revealing the stage, illuminated with soft red hue and smoke fogging the center, giving it an intimate boudoir feel. The scene materialized before the audience feels illicit, exuding a strong provocative vibe. Tyler, with a white button-down, bowtie and suspenders, sleeves rolled up, showcasing his inked forearms, sits by a vast, dark piano. On the other side of the grand piano stands Dante in matching attire, his usually wavy blond hair is slicked back in a sixties fashion. Both men have their eyes trained on Brooklyn who's lying on the piano in a blood red silk dress and matching lipstick. Tyler's fingers caress the keys, bringing the first tunes to fill the grand venue with mystical melody.

Tilting her head up to look at Tyler, Brooklyn's sultry voice seizures the audience, effortlessly collecting their rapt attention to the sensual performance taking place on the stage. Tyler joins her next, broodingly playing the piano, their voices, a collision of smoky and vixen-ish, crooning together seductively. Taking a step toward Tyler, Dante joins the duo, his bass-baritone timbre adds another layer to the song, bringing it to a melodious purity.

No wonder the three of them are considered stars, because what they just created on stage is beyond words. They brought to life a fantasy in a few words, incredible voices and no less persuading performance. They eat the stage up while leaving us all star struck.

As Tyler sings to the keys, his brows pinched, his luring voice making love to the song, Dante sends his hands to Brooklyn's waist, sliding her down from the piano to stand between his thighs. Joining Tyler's voice, Brooklyn lips part, hovering Dante's stubble jaw as they take the duet to an epic climax. Pushing Dante's chest with a sultry hinted smile, Brooklyn saunters seductively toward Tyler who watches her intently.

Halting behind Tyler, Brooklyn slides her hand over his chest while watching Dante who takes control over the sensual song. Brooklyn joins with a mic next to her mouth. She bows a little to reach Tyler's cheek. Tyler cranes his neck to sing into the mic and the three of them take the song to an explosion of voices. Of velvet and smoke and rasp, to an orgy of mesmerizing musical harmony.

Long after the song is over, long after more than a few awards are presented, long after Tyler thanks the crowd for the Singer of the Year award, raising the silver award Jeremy's way with a nod, I still feel like I just woke from an erotic dream. One that leaves me flustered and wanting more. Only a pocking sense of primal jealousy mars this one. What they did on stage was an act, that I'm fully aware of. But the way he looked at her, the way she looked at him … I wish maybe they were a little less gifted at acting. There is a powerful connection between them, one I can't deny. The question is, what does this connection really mean to *my* man.

"Being part of social interactions, especially with adults, helps develop a child's confidence." Jeremy's attempts to stay at the party doesn't help him much.

"Great, then you can do that with Eric when he takes you home, he's an adult." I grin at Jeremy who frowns in return. Seeing how the wheels are still working in his head, I add, "Jer, spare it. It is a school night and we promised your mom you'd be home by ten."

There are a couple more futile attempts to have me change my mind. I got to give it to him, the kid is persistent. Making sure Jeremy is safely buckled in the back seat, I stoop a little to look at him via the window. "Ping me when you get home, okay?"

Jeremy salutes reluctantly, "Yes commander."

"Love you too!"

Eric nods at me from behind the steering wheel, his lips twitched at the side. I nod, mirroring him.

Getting back, I take a detour to freshen up before joining the rest of our gang at the after party taking place in the sky bar on the tenth floor. Glad to find the place vacant, I do a quick makeup check, swiping away a smear of mascara from under my eye. I fluff my hair a little, take a deep breath and try to muster my best acting skills, for pretending doesn't come so natural to me. Some Kool-Aid and a whole lot of nonchalance is in order, otherwise how will I ever be able to appear indifferent to half of the women, and men, in the building lusting over Tyler when I'm the one who chose not to stake my claim, at least not in full display.

"Oh, look what my lucky gods has bestowed upon me."

I roll my eyes. "How are you, Dante?" I direct him a no-nonsense look.

His leering eyes crawl down my body. "Appetizing as ever."

"Great performance tonight." I disregard his refined ways. "All good?"

"Still want to see you come for me." He gives me a look that makes my skin crawl. "What's with the face, doll? C'mon, Ivi, live a little. Be a bad girl … I can help with that." He regards me with a sinful smile which I'm sure would make a lot of women throw themselves at him. This guy is the worst case of looks and ego combined. He has too much of both and he's taking it to the dark side.

Taking the first step to put some distance between us, I say, "I rather be a good girl on the off chance of meeting you later in hell."

He chuckles and it's sexy and creepy at the same time. I shake my head and hurry my steps till I halt in my place. I shake my head. I hate when people do that to me, make me act uncharacteristically, make me say things I usually opt not to say. I exhale through my nose and turn around. Noticing me approach him, Dante's smile turns even cockier.

"Changed your mind, doll?" He offers me his hand. "Bathroom?" Always the cavalier.

Facing him, I drop my hands to my waist. "No. Stop it, okay?" I glare at him. "Why do you do that? I don't get you. You have all this talent, and you're easy on the eyes. But you know what you really are." My glare deepens. "An ass!" "Kurat," I murmur under my breath. "Sad thing is I really believe that deep inside all the douchness you're trying to pull off, there's a cool, kind person. Too bad you're not letting it out more. Maybe for just one night, let people see beyond the image you're trying to portray. I'm not sure what you're looking for, but if it's portraying yourself like a royal prick, then congrats." I clap twice. "You give a great performance, but I'm sure that if you dropped all this assholery you muster so well, people will actually like you even more. Try it out sometime. Being a nice person is actually cool. Give it a shot, you might like it."

His smug smirk morphs into something new, a smile. A simple, normal smile and I must admit that it suits him.

I nod, pleased with myself. "You're going to the party upstairs?"

He nods first, just before his lips tip up. "Maybe the altitude and a little alcohol will loosen you up. Come find me when it happens." He gestures with his hand to the bank of elevators. "After you, Miss Prissy."

I shake my head, pressing the button to call the elevator.

While we wait, Dante looks at me with a new look, as if he's trying to figure me out. "You know, people can have a change of heart."

Thinking he might be considering my little lecture, I give him an interested glance.

"The way she acts around your man," he adds. He raises his eyebrows in tandem to the smirk forming on his lips. Entering the elevator, Dante leans on the wall, eyes never leaving mine. "If you ask me, I say Brooky is ready for some experimenting with Tyler. Reconsider everything, maybe she wants him after all."

"Pardon?"

His smirk grows to my baffled expression. He never explains himself, his focus sidetracks to the cleavage that enters the confined space on the third floor. The bell dings, taking us to the last floor.

Leaving the elevator, I shake off the ninja mind tricking Sir Dante tried to cast on me. I trust Tyler, period. Am I being naïve? Will I regret it later? Time will tell. Tyler hasn't done anything to betray my trust. All along he's been nothing but open and honest with me. What kind of person would I be if I listened to words whispered at my ear with pure malicious intentions? What kind of person would I be if I didn't trust the one person I should?

Abruptly, like magic, the whirlwind of thoughts in my head evaporates. I don't see him first, I feel him. It's enough to have Tyler in the same room making me feel all warm and fuzzy; it's as if he transfers that special feeling by symbiosis. I lift my eyes and he's there, watching me. Waiting for me. I walk over to where Tyler and Jay stand with a small group of people, each with a drink in their hand. I don't know anyone besides Jay, which makes me a bit hesitant at first. Jay introduces me to the group as I join them.

His smile turns wicked when he tips his head at Tyler, "You've met Tyler Lee, right?"

The music in the background is replaced by a calmer tune when Tyler asks if I want to dance. He takes my hand in his, prompting some curious looks from the group and onlookers in our wider radius.

We keep an appropriate distance between our close bodies as we sway to the music. But his warmth, the incredible weight of his hand on my lower back, his scent, being in his orbit just makes me want more. I feel like I can't be close enough to this man. I need to touch him, to feel him, to breathe him in.

"You keep on looking at me like this and I won't be able to hold myself much longer." His words have the opposite effect on me, I should be taking a step back, but instead I lightly caress the nape of his neck where my fingers had crept into his shirt's collar, needing to touch his skin.

"Your performance was mesmerizing," I whisper. Tyler drops his eyes in a humble gesture, only for them to slowly return to my lips, slowly climbing back to my eyes. There are moments when logic disappears. When you're so consumed by your connection to someone that all you see and want is this person in front of you. The need to connect, to get closer, to be lost in him is greater than any other notion. Much more powerful than you. "Tyler," his name funnels through my lips sultry and raspy. "There's nothing I want more than to kiss you right now. What do you say?"

Tyler tips his head, bringing our faces closer, our breaths nearly mixing. "What do I say? I think you know the answer to that. I want the world to know you're mine." He licks his lips as though about to taste me. "Ivi, this relationship is so important to me, I don't even know if you understand how much." His stare deepens. "But it's not about me. *We* come before me, *you* come before me. You decide."

My hands around his neck caress the back of his shorn hair. I stretch on my tiptoes, and deliver my decision by touching my lips to his.

And the world stops.

Finding out what I've done, Tyler's embrace on me tightens in harmony to his mouth fusing with mine as we float into our own universe.

It's all Tyler. All I taste. All I feel. All I could possibly want. And

I don't hear the gasps around us, nor the whispers or the clicks and flashes that follow. I don't hear the avalanche of reactions our kiss has erupted, nor do I hear my anonymity being brutally ripped away from me.

CHAPTER
Ten
CHAPTER

"Brooklyn Mars Storms Out on Tyler Lee Adams Over His Hot Lip-Lock
with an Unidentified Burnette."
"Kiss of Death' for #Brookty's Relationship?"

A couple of "sensational" headlines, out of countless others, on a slew of entertainment news outlets reporting *The Kiss*.

"Nope. Never! Not happening. No contact sports for this guy!" Jeremy points his pointer finger at his chest. "Contact sports can damage your retina!" He huffs with frustration while advocating his choice of "tamer" after-school activities. "It'll mess up my vision for life!" And the kid goes on and on. "Did you know that there are over twelve thousand sports related eye injuries a year among kids up to fourteen. It's crazy, I'm telling you."

About to lecture Mr. Statistics on the importance of regular physical activity, and that there's risk of injury in almost everything in life, I turn to him with a frown of my own. "Hold up, how do you even know these numbers?"

Jeremy sends his tongue to the ice cream cone he's holding and grins at me in his adorable smarty-pants way. "Research conducted by Prevent Blindness of America."

I shake my head, lapping up the plump, pinkish drops trailing down my cone. "Research conducted by Prevent Blindness of America," I echo in a mumble. "Why would you — " I give him another side – glance. "What on earth prompted you to look it up in the first place?"

"Do you even know what lack of proper due diligence and risk assessment can lead to?"

I can't help the smile stretching my lips which is a preamble to an elated snort. I shake my head with so much fondness. This afternoon with Jeremy is exactly what I needed to make it all go away. Bring back normalcy to my life. Bring back innocent little moments of joy. Back to enjoying simplicity and silly, uncomplicated fun.

I know I should have listened to Tyler when he suggested I stay clear of all social media platforms and entertainment news outlets. But I didn't. Curiosity took over me and I just couldn't steer clear. It was there like a healing scab that you're itching to scratch although you're well-aware it'll end up hurting you, or possibly leave you bleeding and scarred. And oh Lord the tailspin it threw me into. I never knew the extant people will go to express their displeasure. Never knew how mean people can actually be. Living my life as I do, I've learned quite fast just how vicious nature can be, how harmful, merciless. I never imagined that some human beings possessed the same qualities. Merciless viciousness.

The media and some (okay, many) of Tyler's, and countless of Brooklyn Mars' fans, simply putting it, are chopping me to pieces. And for the life of me, I don't know why. Or how to handle it. It's not something I was able to prepare myself for. I don't possess the emotional arsenal to defeat it, or avoid it, for that matter. In a way, I'm in an existential panic, lost against this wave of crazy. Of hatred. Why would someone go to the trouble of posting a photoshoped image of me with a knife stuck in my chest is beyond my comprehension.

Funny, I feel so invisible and visible at the same time. I'm everywhere. Literally everywhere, including places I didn't even know existed. Everyone has an opinion about me, but no one knows me! That doesn't deter them from making me someone I'm not or ever will be. All of a sudden, I'm carrying all these labels applied by others. By people who don't know the first thing about me. No, I'm not a Russian plus size model, and no, I'm not that woman Tyler Lee Adams had a kid with, and no, I'm definitely not the reincarnation of everything evil in this world.

I'm just a girl who's very much in love with a man.

Jeremy kicks a pebble we cross on our walk by the shallow water, bringing me back from my bubble of contemplation and brief self-pity party. "Ivi, what's wrong?" empathetic brown eyes regard me.

"Nothing." I muster a smile.

Jeremy shakes his head a little, indicating that he's not sold on my attempt to dismiss it.

"Everything's great." I bump my shoulder with his.

Jeremy twists his mouth, his features contorting. "Is it because of what people are saying about you?"

This kid. Not only is he the smartest little human I've ever met, his emotional maturity is overwhelming. "It's silly, I shouldn't be paying attention to what some people think. They don't really know me, it's just — " I gesture with my hand in dismiss. "It'll go away soon."

"Trolls," Jeremy grunts. A small side-smile touches his lips. "You know I asked my followers on Twitter and Instagram to comment on the mean twits. Check out the hashtag #Iviisthebomb." I look at him in dismay. He grins in return. "I came up with that, cool ah?"

My ribcage expands to contain my swelling heart. "I genuinely love you, kiddo." I give him a side hug, planting a noisy smooch on his temple.

Jeremy pushes his glasses up his nose with one finger. The apples of his cheeks take a rosy hue.

———◆———

As night descends, peeking through dimmed windows, it finds me wrapped up in Tyler's warm embrace, head blissfully rested on his warm, comforting chest. Tyler's fingers leisurely stroke my hair as we watch The Tonight Show. In a low, raspy voice Tyler teases me about having a crush on the show's host. The one time. The one time I mentioned he's cute, Tyler will never let me live it down. I push his chest and look up at him, feigning a frown.

Tyler's lips tip up at the side. "Just keeping track of my competition."

"If I have to keep track of my competitors I'll have to make it my day job, and even then." I give him a cheeky smile.

Tyler doesn't return my smile; his eyes deepen into mine. "You have no competitors, Kiisu."

Sometimes when he says things like that he makes my heart hurt, in the most wonderful way. I inch up to bring my lips to his. Fluttering my eyes closed, I immerse myself in the feeling of being cherished in a slow, soft, sweet kiss. The English word love and its equivalent in Estonian, armastus, meld, becoming one in a slow dance in my head.

A tiny snore from the sofa next to us prompts us to break the kiss with unified smiles. We tilt our heads with matching adoring expressions to look at Jeremy in his pajamas as he scrunches his nose and lets out another cute snore. I sit up and gently pull his glasses from his nose, fold them, and set them on the low table.

"I'd better get him to bed," Tyler says still adorning a magnificent caring expression.

I pull my pink knee-high socks up and hug my thighs to my chest as I watch Tyler carry Jeremy up the stairs. Jeremy's head is slumped over Tyler's shoulder, Tyler's strong arms around him, and the duet of words expressing love in my head take on brighter colors.

———— ♦ ————

Brushing his teeth, shirtless and absorbed, Tyler watches me through the bathroom mirror. With my own toothbrush stuck in my mouth, I give him a questioning look. He spits out into the sink and wipes his mouth with a towel. I can't believe he makes even this banal act … sexy. I really need to have my head examined, normal people don't swoon over spittle!

Tyler is focused on me. "Am I going to lose you over this?"

"Wha?" I ask with the toothbrush still in my mouth. I take it out, confused. "Lose me? What are you talking about?"

Tyler takes a couple of steps to reach me. He sends his hand to my hair, moving it behind my shoulders. He cuddles my cheeks, crouching a little to align our stares. "You haven't been yourself since it all began. Should I be concerned, are you going to run away?"

I sigh. "Yeah, it's too much in a way. I feel like I'm becoming someone I don't want to be, someone who cares about what other people are saying. Someone vulnerable. I need to be me, and this situation makes it hard. I feel like I'm in a show. I hate pretending. I hate what's running through my head. I hate that I let the situation seed a sense of insecurity in me."

"Look at me, Kiisu," he says in a gentle voice. "After all, it's you and me, everything around us is just noise. You and me, nothing else matters. I'm yours completely. I belong to you with everything that I am. Please don't get side blinded by this chaos. This life, in a way, cost me too much already. I lost some good years with Jeremy, *you* … I'm not letting you get away. I don't want *you* to be my one that got away."

I bite on my lip and softly shake my head. "Tyler, I'm not running away. All of this doesn't change how I feel about you. I'm not going to lie and say that I'm not affected by it." I blink. The intensity of his stare is overpowering. "It's not what I expected, and I feel a bit …" I take a deep breath. "A bit lost. A lot overwhelmed. It's hard to compute this thing when you're not used to it. I guess I'll get used to it somehow… eventually. And there's nothing I want to be more than yours."

Tyler regards me intently. "I'm sorry." He sighs.

I shake my head once more. "You don't have to be. *I'm not sorry*, I wouldn't change a thing. If this is a part of the package of having you then I'll take it as it is." I can't help but wonder, for how long as I hear the words leave my mouth? For how long can I endure so much negativity and… hatred.

His response is holding me tight to his chest. Tilting back to look at me, he leans in to softly kiss my lips. Breaking apart, Tyler stays with me as I apply my night lotion and brush my hair.

"There's a — " He starts, winces and sighs. I search his eyes via the mirror. His brows pinch. "There are a few public events, with the release of the movie, the soundtrack and all — " He scratches his neck over the tattoo I love dearly. "Do you want to … you don't need to, but, will you be joining me?"

I stop, the brush halting halfway down my head. "Umm. I guess?" I can't mask the agitation the idea brings.

Tyler bites on his cheek. He nods a couple of times, contemplating. "How about you join me at the last two events, in Europe, after you're back from Nepal."

I nod. When his words actually sink in, I gape at him. "Nepal?"

He rewards me with a soft smile. "You wanted to be there for the school's opening thing, didn't you?"

I blink at him, holding my breath.

His smile widens. "Got you a ticket."

I squeal and jump at him. Tyler catches me with a chuckle. I pepper kisses all over his neck and amused face. "Wow. That means so much! You have no idea. How can I ever thank you?"

He tips back to grin at me with enough naughtiness to melt my insides. Grabbing a hunk of my butt, he rasps, "I have a few ideas. No better time to show your appreciation than now."

I giggle, planting another kiss on his lips. A kiss that gathers momentum like wildfire … sparking gasoline.

Eleven

"An over-indulgence of us, even though it's magical, intoxicates me, baby."
"Remove the Spell" One of Tyler Lee Adams' old, instant hits that Ivi has
lately been obsessing over.

L ittle tingles of excitement fizz around in my chest, rapidly increasing as I see some familiar faces light up with joy at the sight of me as I make my way up the path to the camp. An ear-piercing yelp has us all turn to a wildly grinning Renata who's running my way with arms open wide. In less than thirty minutes or so I feel like I never left, reconnecting with some of the volunteers I met before and new arrivals. Genuine friendliness transpires from everyone, people I've known for a while and complete strangers that within the shortest time become new friends. It never ceases to amaze me how these missions tend to bring together people who'd never had a chance to meet in any other circumstances and make them friends for life. Form an incredible bond, its significance hard to put into words.

Renata, not so stealthily, drags me away from the joined lunch break to catch up by ourselves. How easily she manages to elicit carefree laughter out of me is something that comes as a surprise. The last couple of weeks have made me a little more guarded, a little more closed-up, a whole lot un-me. It feels wonderful to be in a place where no one judges you, where no one looks at you through a magnifying glass, where you're not media sensationalism. A sudden epiphany startles me, leaving me utterly baffled. Why am I this glad to be away, from L.A., from gossip, from the circus around me? Maybe after all … it's not the right place for me?

Taking a huge breath to clear my mind, I focus back on my friend. I play along with an amused smile, collaborating with the third degree about my life in L.A. She gives me a bit of a hard time about keeping the whole Tyler thing quiet on my last visit, but it's all in good spirits. When Renata jokingly, or not, asks if I have naked photos of Tyler on my phone that's where I draw the line and put the kibosh on the "friendly sharing," declaring, "Enough about me, what have you been up to?"

And the dam breaks.

I'm flooded with information, poured at me in a sing songy accent and an abundance of Brazilian sass. I'm having a hard time keeping up with the tidbits torrent, that is until Renata's line of thought seems to short, followed by a softening in her entire demeanor. I frown at the rose hue climbing up her sharp cheekbones. I turn back, following her gaze, to encounter a fine looking golden-haired superman. Short seconds later I'm introduced to Mikael Sandström, the camp's latest Swedish delight addition. Not missing a beat, Nordic Superman reaches Renata and plants a far from being arctic kiss on my utterly swooned friend.

Mikael turns out to be a soft spoken and, simply put, great guy. Mikael, who seems to have been glued to Renata's right side, tells me about how they met, shy of a month ago. "I swear, I was sure she was about to bite my hand off." He laughs, kissing her temple along the way. I listen with an amused expression as he elaborates, telling me how innocently he'd taken Renata's dinner bowl by mistake, an incident that almost cost him his life.

"I was famished." She shrugs. "It was the longest day, we worked through lunch to finish the wood floor in the school, and like I said, I was famished." She gestures cheekily at Mikael. "And this one comes up and takes my dinner."

Mikael makes a frightened expression. "She was scary." Renata rolls her eyes. "Until I smiled at her."

"No, sir, it wasn't until you gave me back my food." Renata frowns at her boyfriend. Turning to me with her hand next to her mouth, she loudly whispers, "It's was totally the smile."

When night descends over the camp to the soundtrack of crickets' chirping, I'm standing by the fire, handing out bowls of steaming Kitchari. My muscles ache and I can smell the day's labor soaked in my clothes as I take a seat on a makeshift bench made of a piece of wood and a few blocks, next to some new volunteers. Renata and Mikael join when I put down my bowl to cuddle a mug of tea in my hands. Blowing on the hot beverage, I listen to my friend as she tells me about some short and long-term plans.

The long one involves a road trip she's planning with Mikael right after the opening ceremony of the school. The shorter one, which apparently includes me, is visiting another camp, an hour away, tomorrow. "They need some extra help to prepare stocks of medical equipment for the Doctors Without Borders mobile clinics."

I immediately agree even though a long ride up the mountains in one of the old trucks we have at our disposal is not something I'm eager to repeat.

I'm exhausted when I finally lay my head on the hard, slim pillow, but not tired enough to try and call Tyler after missing four calls from him earlier. Reaching his voicemail, I decide to call it a night. However, my curiosity gets the better of me, and I use my satellite phone to check the web for the latest on me, hopping with all my heart that the hype has subsided, even a little.

The first result that catches my eyes has my heart skip a beat. Under a headline stating that Tyler and I broke up and something about Brooklyn Mars' fans thrilled at the "unification" there's a photo that makes my stomach drop like there's no gravity. I'm having a hard time swallowing as I study the photo of Tyler and Brooklyn walking out of a theater venue together. Tyler's in a tuxedo, his blazer draped over Brooklyn's lean shoulders. Her face is tilted upwards with a soft smile trapped between her teeth while Tyler, his lips set in a warm smile, gently kisses her temple. What pains me the most, besides them looking perfect together, is Tyler's expression is identical to the way he looks at me ... or used to look at me. They look happy, and intimate, and connected, the exact way some of my deepest fears have concocted this nightmare, that Tyler would be just like that with someone else.

He's never even told you he loves you, my spiteful insecurity mocks me. Jealousy is a beast of an emotion, one that's hard to eradicate, especially when it stretches its malicious claws to grab every sensible cell in your brain. Even though it pains me to look at the photo I can't make myself stop. It feels like a betrayal, the way he looks at her, the gentleness in his features as he touches his lips to her hair. I'm confused and sadden as I finally switch off the phone and toss it inside my bag. Tyler might be an amazing human, after all, he is a human, however sometimes the best of intentions simply aren't enough, right?

After some deep introspection, just before I fall asleep, I promise myself not to jump to conclusions, but to instead talk to Tyler. After all, there are three sides to every story. The mountain of crap you run in your head, his side (that attempts to soothe you,) and ... the truth.

CHAPTER

Twelve

CHAPTER

"If only feelings had an off switch."
A thought that swims around Ivi's head throughout the day.

step out to the open kitchen fresh and clean — well, more like fresh-ish and clean-ish. Fresh-ish (didn't have the best night sleep. You see, a photo of your boyfriend looking utterly in love with someone else might do that to a girl,) and clean-ish (well, it's something you get used to —never really being completely clean in this place, an outside hose-shower might do that to a girl.)

Slowly, still in waking up rhythm, I make my way to grab a morning tea and join my friends. We take our time having our porridge and drinking our hot beverages while talking to the rest of the group.

The delegation of volunteers headed to help the Doctors Without Borders staff isn't big enough to fill up the old truck. There are just a few of us, the rest stay to finish the last touches for the school. Not too enthusiastic about yet another bumpy ride, I make my way to the truck with a light backpack on my shoulder for an overnight stay. Biting my lip, I contemplate running back to the room to take my phone with me. I know it's not the most mature thing to do, not being available to talk to Tyler, still…

"Hey, Ivi, in this lifetime!" Renata calls from the back of the truck, snuggled to Mikael's side.

I nod, smiling, quickly deciding that a little breather from Tyler is the right thing for me right now. I leave the phone behind, hopefully together with the feeling my heart is laden by.

Drinking in the breathtaking, wild scenery, I push away disturbing thoughts and pledge to focus on everything else but Tyler for the next twenty-four hours. Ready for what the day will bring along.

And it brings so much. For the most part, I feel like I'm sinking under its weight, working harder than ever.

Night finds us exhausted. I feel like I've run a marathon as I shrug on a woolly sweater before joining the large group congregated around a vast fire pit. I can feel my lower back and the tension in my thighs as I bend to take a seat next to Maya, an Israeli medic I was teamed up with for the day.

"You guys saved us today," she says, handing me a bowl. The scent of hearty, spicy lentil soup engulfs me as I cradle the bowl in my hands, seeking to warm myself up. I nod with a gentle smile in response, finally letting my body indulge in the simple act of resting. Carrying equipment, moving it from location to location, setting up examination areas, it's been a busy day, to put it mildly.

Easy conversations spark in little groups as dinner is passed around and people let themselves finally relax. A slight shiver runs up my spine as a breeze of icy wind penetrates my sweater. In short moments it feels like a powerful cold front with Arctic air is descending upon us. Robert, one of the senior doctors, jogs toward us from the main house. Seeming to catch his breath, he addresses everyone around him. "There's a cyclone warning."

Surprised questions and mumbles come as a response from the people around me.

"We need to take shelter immediately. I don't want to take any risks. Please get inside as soon as possible," he says, looking pointedly at the crowd of volunteers, waiting for us to follow his order.

Not a moment later, heavy rain pours from the sky, prompting us to do as told.

Trying to get our minds off the disconcerting sounds of havoc coming from outside, we play cards and board games, some read or just fall into conversations with others as wild winds and rain plummet the windows persistently.

We wake up to a sunny day, a complete contrast to the night before. At a morning briefing I learn that in other villages there's damage to some buildings and dwellings, and that the massive landslides have left much of the district with limited or no road access. Meaning, we're stuck here for the near future. "It could take a couple of days or a week, we still need to assess the damage." I hear someone beside me explain to his fellow volunteer.

The next couple of days pass with even harder work, damage control and constant thoughts of Tyler and how much I miss him. It feels like he rented a chunk of real estate in my brain which he never intends to leave.

CHAPTER
Thirteen
CHAPTER

Tyler

I eye the guitar on my lap with a deep frown. I rub my bristled cheeks with two hands, forcing whatever is coming over me to go away. It's this niggling feeling poking at me somewhere inside my head. A feeling I can't decipher, nor push away.

"Hey Da — Tyler, check this one out." Jeremey, sitting at the control desk in the studio, grins my way. He holds the guitar I got him a while ago in one hand, his other hovering over the mouse on the desk.

It became our thing, once a week when he visits. I teach him how to play the guitar. Let's just say, I'm grateful for my offspring's other talents. This kid probably won't be following in his dad's footsteps. Come to think about it, taking after his mom would be a better choice anyhow. An artist versus an academic. It's a no-brainer. However, if I'm being honest, once he finds out about the phenomenon that is a woman, well, the singer card would help better there.

A smile that comes from deep inside warms me, the same effect it has each time my kid almost calls me dad. The last thing I'd do is push him, he's been through a lot because of me, but I'd love for this word to fall naturally from his lips. I couldn't be more grateful for this outcome, him and me, so naturally hanging out. Him being a part of my life is something I'm still overwhelmed by. Thank fucking Christ for second chances. And for an unbelievably awesome kid.

Jeremy snickers, watching me as I read the meme he motioned at. I roll my eyes while shaking my head, which of course just elevates his amusement. Jeremy grins wider, saying, "If it's on the internet it must be true."

I hide my smile, looking down at my guitar. Seems like the kid can't get enough of ridiculing me for moronic lists like this one — "Hottest Men" where I'm ranked number one.

"We have something better to do, here." With the guitar pick between my lips I tip my chin at the guitar in his arm.

Still grinning, Jeremy scrolls down, looking at some recent images related to me. "Maybe there's something on me," he murmurs next.

"I'd rather there not be *anything* on you. Trust me kid, you don't want to find yourself on the internet," I say, then add, "Hey, Jer, I'm serious."

Jeremy nods, his attention still on the screen. I shake my head, glancing at my son and the screen. "Hold up," I say abruptly.

Jeremy observes the image that caught my eye and turns to me, the smile slowly slips from his lips.

I inhale deeply through my nose, contemplating the image of Brooklyn and me looking… intimate. I cringe at the caption below the image: Tyler Lee Adam's True Love, The One Person He Looks at This Way. This moment was indeed intimate, however, how it's portrayed on the large monitor tells a completely different story to anyone who wasn't with us in that moment. A moment when I told Brook how I feel about Ivi, how overwhelmingly strong it is, and she told me she couldn't be happier for me.

Jeremy turns to me, his clever eyes somewhat hesitant. He frowns, "I read earlier today that the weather condition in Nepal is getting worse." His gentle way of bringing up Ivi after the photo he'd just seen. "I hope Ivi is okay."

My voice is raspier as I say, "I'll try calling her again." Again. Ivi has been unreachable for more than a day now. That niggling feeling in me just multiplied.

As though to emphasize his point, Jeremy turns to check the weather update for the area in Nepal where Ivi is staying.

I'm still deep in thought when the accord of his voice alone startles me. "Dad, they say that a hurricane just hit the Sindhupalchok region." It feels like a brick hit my stomach as he adds, "People are missing, two are dead, and thousands are without power."

CHAPTER
Fourteen

"Thud. Thud. Thud." Ivi's heart upon her return to the camp.

A few rays of sun welcome us as we finally leave the building, they shine bright — somewhat sardonically — illuminating the chaos of broken branches and debris on the ground. Compared to past weather damage, what's revealed before us is a pleasing aftermath, if it can be called that. Buildings and structures stayed firmly intact versus anything that wasn't firmly secured to the ground being brutally shuffled around along with a small car and a roof that was torn off by the wild winds. I'm more than thankful that it's more of a mess than a bona fide disaster, but this is just this village. I can't help but worry about our village, its residents, and our fellow volunteers.

For a couple of hours before taking a ride back to camp, we partake in an impromptu ceremony that the locals hold to show their gratitude for the outcome. This attitude warms my heart. Instead of fuelling thoughts of misfortune and woes due to the tragedies that strike so often, they choose to show gratitude. I'm humbled by these people. I can't help but wonder how sometimes those who are blessed by fortune, satiated from everything life bestows on them, are the ones that at the first sight of calamity lose all faith.

Shortly after the quick service, we help in uncluttering the area so the makeshift clinic can resume its work.

Just before noon as the sky darkens once again, I pull my backpack up my shoulder, rub dust off my hands and climb up the back of the truck. We're silent throughout the ride, some too exhausted to communicate and others in a contemplative mood. When a chilled breeze hits us, I shrug on my sweatshirt. When rain follows there's nothing for us to do in the exposed bed of the truck but cover ourselves with a flimsy plastic sheet that does a lousy job in protecting us from getting drenched. At a certain point I just give up and let the rain wash over me.

We find the camp bustling, and thankfully mostly unscathed. There is an undercurrent of buzzing energy, as we park in front of Big Mom's house. The rain lets out, replaced by the sun again, however I'm soaked to my bones from the long ride and the only thing I can think of is changing into dry clothes. With my head bowed, lightly shivering, I hop off the tailgate. "Be right back, I need to get rid of these clothes," I murmur to Renata, and with utter determination make my way to the house. A strange vibe coming from the improvised scaffolding embracing the freshly varnished school prompts me to divert my focused from my path. I'm taken aback by the odd scene. Every single person that just left the truck is frozen in place, their attention trained at something near the school. Squinting my gaze, I search for the root cause.

I do a double take and nearly fall back on my bum to the vision that in my head seems like a fata morgana. I'm glued to my spot, utterly perplexed, watching Tyler — my Tyler, in a simple black hoodie, distressed jeans and heavy boots, as he walks my way. His eyes, their familiarity, their warmth, trained on me.

And the entire world, complete with my ability to do anything but be wholly pulled toward him, is gone. Everything that happened since the time I last saw him flies out of my mind. I'm solely Tyler-cognizant. Drama, painful to watch portrayals, wounded hearts, natural disasters, all vanished by one loaded stare. It's just him.

My breath is trapped somewhere in my chest as I wait for him to reach me. It's not a game of power, letting him come to me. The thing is, I couldn't move even if I wanted. Tyler's hand reaches me first by cupping my cheek. An involuntary shiver runs through me, even my body is too overwhelmed to control itself. Next, as I'm still realizing that the image in front of me is indeed him and not a figment of my imagination, I'm bundled in the warmest of embraces and that's when I finally exhale. Finally everything feels just right.

Tyler presses a kiss to the center of my head, murmuring through a relieved sigh, "You're fine." His hug on me tightens for some prolonged moments, pressing me to the center of his warmth.

He pulls back to look at me. Assessing my baffled expressions, his lips tip up mischievously. "Are you always this soaked, or are you just happy to see me?"

I let out a humored snort. Shaking my head, I say, "Lame." His eyes light up playfully and his smile widens, calling for his dimple to pop out. "What are you doing here?" I ask next.

"You didn't answer my calls."

Right, if someone doesn't answer your calls you just hop on a plane and fly for about twenty hours to see them. Yeah, makes sense. In his world maybe.

"I was worried. Especially after the reports that came in after the cyclone." He nods his head, extenuating his words. "Majorly worried."

I watch him closely for a beat, processing.

He dips his chin, bringing his lips to my ear. "Now that I know that you're okay, and I finally have you in my arms, can I at least get a happy-to-see-you kiss?" He grins at me.

Mirroring his smile, I lean toward him and stop as reality sinks in to the sound of the people loitering around us. I steal a glance around me to find my friends appearing to mind their own business, but not really. They are way too obvious. Looks like Renata is about to pull out a director's chair and get a camera rolling.

I squeeze Tyler's hand, tipping my face in the direction of our audience, "Maybe in a slightly more private spot."

"Maybe?" He cocks his head with a boyish smile.

I point my finger at him. "Stop doing your wooer Jedi mind tricks on me, wait with the charm till I can reciprocate."

Tyler chuckles. He motions with his hand, animated eyes on me. "Lead the way to privacy, Kiisu."

Tyler links our fingers, following me en route to Big Mom's house. Softly speaking, he asks me about the last couple of days. "Sometimes it feels like bad luck is a reoccurring thing around here. I just wish these people could get a break." I tell him all about the insanity that left, once more, chaos in this place when loud whispers reach us. I halt, my mouth snaps into a flat line as the voices become clearer. "Isn't he with that other super famous person, Brooklyn something? Oh, Mars. Brooklyn Mars!" A glowing snap of that infamous intimate photo of Brooklyn and Tyler from a few days ago conjures in my mind's eye. Not the pause of my step, nor the drop of my hand from his is something I'm aware of, for all my resources go to trying to ease the painful squeeze in my heart.

"Ivi?" Tyler's concerned, low voice comes from a step ahead as he turns to me.

I inhale deeply and slowly look up. Meeting his gaze takes a great effort.

He drops his head and slowly lifts it up to look at me, "Look." His jaw clenches as he seems to consider something. He shakes his, looking irate … with himself. I watch him inquisitively as he sends his hand to the back of his jeans and fetches a satellite phone. Glancing at his watch, he twists his mouth in exasperation. With eyebrows pinched, he looks at me, "have you seen that last photo of Brooklyn and —?"

I nod accent even before he finishes the sentence.

He exhales through his nose, scratching his stubble. "I — " he starts and stops. His features morph with determination, "Fuck this." I watch him, startled at his indecisive, odd behavior, as he searches up a contact on his phone and brings it to his ear, his troubled eyes on mine.

"Hey," he says to the person on the line. "Yeah, sorry, I know it's late, but I need you to talk to Ivi right now and explain — " he nods, "Yeah, *that*." Listening, he nods once more. "Appreciate it, B."

Tyler retrieves the phone from his ear and offers it to me. "It's Brooklyn, can you talk to her for me?"

Somewhat anxious, I take the phone from Tyler. Casting down my stare, fidgeting with my shoe in the gravel, I say, "Hi, it's Ivi."

"Hi Ivi, ummm, we've met before. We don't know each other too well, I'm Tyler's. Ummm, I — " An uncertain Brooklyn Mars begins. I swallow hard, not too enthusiastic about Brooklyn being Tyler's whatever. The "belonging" part doesn't bode well. "Listen Ivi, Tyler is *very* important to me, and I wouldn't be doing this for anyone else on the planet. What I'm about to tell you, I need you to keep under wraps, honor my privacy."

"Sure," I murmur, having a hard time following.

She clears her throat. "Tyler and I, we've been friends forever and he's a person that I blindly trust and since he feels the same way about you…" The silence that comes next makes me think she's culling her words carefully. Her next words come out quick as a gunshot. "Ivi, I'm gay."

"Pardon?" I croak out, puzzled.

"I'm queer, Ivi," she says on an exhale. "And it's something that

I'm not inclined to share with the world for the time being." Her tone is harsher. "You got a taste of our world by now, and well, you know how judgmental and intrusive it can get."

I hum assent, still genuinely baffled.

"Till now, Tyler has been a great friend by helping me stay clear of any suspicion by playing hot and cold about our relationship with the media. But now, now that he has you, and I know just how important you are to him, I know we can't do that anymore. I understand. We're still very close and I wouldn't give up our friendship for anything."

Not even once has Tyler lied to me from the very beginning. There was nothing going on between him and Brooklyn besides true friendship. Tyler is as great as I always thought he was, and apparently even more.

"Thank you for sharing that with me, Brooklyn. I truly appreciate it. I know it wasn't easy. And be assured, I won't compromise the trust you've given me."

"He's the best, you're a lucky woman, Ivi."

"I know."

I hand Tyler his phone. He takes it from me, his eyes searching mine. I send him a tender smile. His reciprocating, relived boyish smile almost splits my heart in two. How can someone encompass so much into a simple gesture? His way of reaching me and telling me everything I want to hear without a word is incomprehensible. I thread our fingers together again and wordlessly start toward Big Mom's home.

We walk in silence, our hands linked. We enter the house in silence. We take the stairs up in silence. We close the door behind us in silence.

My heart drums in my chest and it feels like electric currents roam along my skin as we walk toward each other in slow steps. The short, loaded seconds before our lips touch are full of excruciating anxiety.

CHAPTER
Fifteen

"It's easier expressing yourself with lyrics and musical notes, believe me, it's much easier than intimately opening up to another human. My music will probably tell you more about me than I could ever say about myself."
Tyler Lee Adams in an interview for Billboard.

At this point in my life I feel like I've seen it all. I feel like I can't so easily be caught off-guard. Like I'm in charge of my mental clarity together with my emotions.

I know how amazing Tyler is. There's no doubt about it. But sometimes he does things that do catch me completely off guard. Leave me shell-shocked and stupidly heart-eyed dazed. Sometimes it feels like Tyler, unconsciously perhaps, controls the needle of my emotional compass. I watch him from under the bonfire's dancing flames, my lips in an easy, blissful tilt. Tyler's eyes shine with mirth as he, once again, fails to mimic the song the local kids are trying to teach him. Raj breaks into cute laughter when Tyler, strumming on the guitar, sings the Nepali nursery rhyme with the heaviest American accent, ridiculously twisting the words. My uncontrollable happy laughter is a product of the sweet scene taking place before me.

Grinning at them, Tyler points at his chest, "Now me, okay?" A dozen pairs of animated young eyes watch him. At Tyler's attempt to change the song, little shorn heads shake with disapproval. When they start fussing in Nepali, Tyler holds his arms up in surrender, "Okay, okay," he says through a chuckle. "Bossy bunch, aren't ya?"

Long moments later when the kids finally let Tyler take a break, he joins me and a few other volunteers for some tea. So easily Tyler finds his place with these people, as if he were with us from the very beginning. I'm more than grateful that my fellow volunteers don't give him any special treatment. From time to time there is some staring and occasional whispers, but nothing too obvious otherwise. No one has pulled out a phone for a selfie thus far, which I declare a success. Even Renata seems to curb her enthusiasm.

A couple of teas and some crumbly oat cookies later, Tyler and Mikel drown the campfire with water and then move on to mix the ashes and embers with soil as Renata and I collect the leftovers from the meal and bring it to two guys at the washing station. Not long after people file out for the night.

Not long after, it's just him and me.

———◆———

I let out an animated snort, watching Tyler as he stands in my room, which my roommates were kind enough to desert for the night. To me, he looks entirely out of place. Not to mention how the room seems to shrink by his presence. "You couldn't look more out of place if you tried, Mr. Adams."

He raises his eyebrows in question.

Hardly containing my amusement, I mimic Robin Leach's voice, declaring, "Being displaced from the glitz and glam of his L.A. home leads this world renowned singer to contemplate one of life's most pressing questions: how do common humans live?"

Slowly stepping toward me as he shakes his head, murmuring, "Kiisu, Kiisu, Kiisu — those who play with fire get burned."

I narrow my eyes at him, licking my lips. "Tyler, Tyler, Tyler." I add a little breathy shade and a zest of colorful sass to my voice. "Can't wait for you to set me on fire."

Tyler throws me half a smile right before grabbing me by my waist and lifting me to straddle him. The close feel of him against my widely spread legs robs me of my bantering abilities. Grabbing my butt, Tyler presses me against him. "You were saying," he mutters to my collarbone while tasting it.

Dropping my head back, I whisper, "Fire."

Gears shift in no time. Gentle nuzzling morphs into frantic kissing. With a groan that powders my belly with heat Tyler walks us till we clash with the wall, making a noticeable thud. Big Mom's house is so flimsy that it feels like a 7.5 magnitude earthquake hit the building. I sober up, realizing just how obvious the noises we're making are to our fellow tenants. "Tyler," I blurt out of breath, drawing back.

Grinding against me, lips just under my earlobe, Tyler grunts incoherently.

"Tyler, we can't." I gently push his chest.

Adorably frowning, Tyler lifts his drunken eyes to mine.

Cupping his warm cheeks, I plant a chaste kiss on his moist lips, already mourning the loss of his delicious attack. "We can't, these walls are paper-thin. A tiny sneeze can be heard throughout the house."

Looking sweetly determined Tyler dismisses my protest with, "We'll be quiet."

I have to send my hand to his chin to remove his lips that in a millisecond magnetize to my cleavage. I gently force his face up and shake my head. "Rain check?" I go for cute. Cute doesn't seem to work that well this time. Tyler isn't the jolliest camper as he reluctantly sets me down.

It's hard enough coaxing Tyler to a copulation timeout, sweet talking him to a separate bed arrangement is a vain attempt. That's how we find ourselves facing each other with barely a sliver of space between us in one of the narrow, hard beds.

Conversing in soft tones, eyes deep in one another, I lightly stroke Tyler's fingers. "I love the new lyrics you wrote." I tell him.

"Had great inspiration," he smiles at me in this intimate darkness.

Not being able to touch him like I want to makes an unyielding desire run through me, shooting currents down my belly. Forbiddance is an erotic poison.

"Your writing is so unique, it's like magic — with just a few words you manage to tell an entire story." I refer to lyrics that he's been working on that he shared with me earlier.

"At first, all I heard was the riff. The lyrics came later," he says. "In a way it's my own view of the past few months, Jeremy and you entering my life. When I write and it all aligns — when these little moments happen ... When what I feel deep inside shines through and it resonates with other people it's such a rewording feeling. In a way, I'm connecting with others through my songs."

I'm listening to him, my eyes closely following the way his lips move, the cadence of his eyes as he looks at me. As deeply as I'm absorbed in Tyler's words, I find myself distracted, processing the messages his tone and warm body that gradually connects with mine, transmit.

I swallow hard, "Tyler," I whisper. "You just shivered."

His eyes are trained on mine as he whispers back in a low, loaded voice, "Yeah, that's how much I want you."

Tilting my head up, I press a warm kiss on his lips because I need to, because there's nothing on this planet I want to do more than connect with this man, in every possible way I can. Our finger pads touch as we slowly scoot a little closer. And closer. Pressed alongside each other, our skin burns from under our light attire. Our kisses grow hotter and determined and it feels like he's doing what he taunted me with earlier, setting me on fire.

My resolve to practice celibacy tonight shades off with every piece of garment we peel off our burning bodies.

CHAPTER
Sixteen

"I want that in my life."

"What, a mega gorgeous rock star? Yeah, sign me up for that too."

"No, it's not about who he is, it's about how he looks at her.

That. I want that."

A hushed conversation between two younger volunteers as they sneak

glances at Tyler and Ivi at breakfast.

"You sure you want to do this? you really don't have to — "

"Kiisu, hand me the brush." Tyler extends his hand in request, politely telling me to can it already.

A smile stretches my lips because A. he really doesn't have to do this. B. he's such an awesome human. C. it's sort of amusing to watch *the* Tyler Lee Adams dabble with manual labor. And D. he's such an awesome human. "Knock yourself out, Mr. Adams," I tease, handing him one of the paintbrushes sticking out from my cargo back pockets. I shake my head in affectionate amusement, chewing on a Big Red.

"What's so funny, miss Kert?" Tyler asks, his smiling eyes focused on my grin.

I grin wider. "You."

It's Tyler's turn to shake his head in amusement. He steps closer to me, sending his hand to cup my cheek. He tilts my head up and leans in to touch his lips to mine, still smiling. As an instinct my lips part to his.

Frowning, I gape at him a moment later. "No, you didn't just — "

Tyler chuckles, making a whole production of chewing the gum he just hijacked from me in pretense of a kiss. "Get to work, Kiisu. Stop fooling around." Utterly pleased with himself, Tyler grabs one of the paint cans from the pyramid of cans next to the scaffolding surrounding the school and takes a place by the wall, ready to help with the last coat of varnish.

I'm happy. Truly happy. Having Tyler around, here, in this place that humbles me and makes me feel so fulfilled just amplifies it all. Having this person that's so special to me share this part of my life with me is not something I ever thought would happen. I'm overwhelmed by how happy it makes me to be able to share it with him. I send Tyler a goofy, I'm deeply gaga for you glance and climb to the second step of the scaffolding to reach the same height Tyler easily reaches from the ground.

We stroke the brushes along the wooden wall while Tyler hums an unfamiliar tune and I contemplate the shortening to-do list I have to complete before going back home tomorrow evening.

Steps crunching gravel pull me out of my painting meditation. "Ivi, can you give me a hand in the kitchen, just until Iva gets back. She should be back soon. I just don't want to delay lunch. You know how cranky some of them get when food takes time." Renata rolls her eyes.

I smile. "Sure, no problem." I set my brush on the can and jump off the scaffolding.

I turn to Tyler who's watching me with a clandestine smile, looking like he's contemplating something. Something that has to do with me.

I cock my head in question. In response, Tyler's tender smile deepens, his brows pinched somewhat enigmatic. For a prolong moment he just stares at me with this sweet, unfathomable expression. "Go on, I'll wait here."

With an easy conversation, I help with the food, slicing bread, stirring some soup while Renata sets out plates and cutlery for when the expected throng of hardworking, hungry people arrive. In no time Iva returns and I get back to Tyler.

Tyler watches me, yet again with that look as I take the final step to join in.

"All good?" I ask attempting to climb back on the scaffolding.

"All good," he echoes, eyes glued to me.

Something is going on with him. I'm unable to decode the encrypted vibe he's emitting and even though it looks to be positive it unsettles me. When I have my two feet on the second step and the brush back in my hand, I turn to Tyler about to ask, I'm not sure what I'm about to ask because the look in his eyes causes a short in my brain.

Tyler is turned my way, he seems tense. From where I stand it looks like a multitude of emotions cross his face. His lips tip at the side but he doesn't really smile, it's a wobbly attempt at smiling. His lips part to speak. I'm so focused on him it feels like the tension he harbors made its way to me because suddenly, I'm stiff and nervous.

His eyes run over me, from my work boots, up my faded cargos to the fleece hoodie to my neck, mouth, wary stare. "I love you."

Stunned, I lose my bearings and fall back flat on my butt with a strangled yelp. I rub my rear looking up at Tyler who's making a crap job of trying to hold back laughter.

He drops to his hunches next to me. With the sweetest of amused boyish smiles, he asks, "You okay?"

I nod, still unable to form words.

He sends his hand to tuck a lock of hair behind my ear that due to the fall covers my eye. Resting both elbows on his thighs, still squatting, his eyes capture mine. "So, here's the thing."

All I can do is blink.

"You remember the day you left me when we were in the back of my car saying good-bye?"

My brows wrinkle, and I nod. "Yes, Tyler, I do." I wait for him to go on, utterly dazzled.

"There's something I never told you about that day." Tyler strokes my face with his stare.

I keep looking up at him, swallowing hard.

"Well, while you were kissing me like it was the last time you'd ever do that, I fell so deeply in love with you. Felt like you were taking my heart with you when you left."

"Tyler," comes out on an emotional whisper.

Tyler stands, offering me his hand. He pulls me up close to him. Threading his fingers through either side of my face he tips his face close to mine. "I am in awe of you. You amaze me and wreck me at the same time. You're the most caring and unique women I've ever met. I love you, Kiisu."

I'm choked up with emotions. "I love you too."

Just before wrapping me in the warmest embrace, Tyler tilts my head up, and presses his lips to mine in a tender, lingered kiss.

———◆———

"I'm so excited," I tell Tyler as we make our way from the kitchen where we had breakfast to the impromptu opening ceremony a group of the volunteers arranged last night when the school was finally declared complete. "Can't wait to see their faces when they see what we've done inside."

"You guys should be proud of yourselves. You've done such a great job." Tyler squeezes my waist, and leaves a kiss on my forehead.

A humble grin softens my lips. Some people join us as we take the path to the school.

Renata's rolling laughter joins mine as we notice that even though there's a red fabric with a bow at the main door waiting to be officially cut, some of the kids already found their way inside.

"Little nuggets," Renata says though a wide grin.

Sounds of joy and hurried steps come out from the building. Sounds of joy. This, this is exactly what makes the hard work worth it. Helping people, bringing them up from their hardest falls. Putting smiles on kids' lips and joy in their hearts. I'm washed with satisfaction.

I rest my hand on Tyler's abs, calling for his attention. Tyler dips his chin to look at me. "Remember that generous check you gave me on Christmas?" I gesture my free hand at the school. "We wouldn't have been able to complete this without it."

Tyler nods in a humble way. "I'm glad I could help."

It's a quaint ceremony, if one can call it that. Some volunteers say a few words. Big Mom and a couple of parents thank us with broken English and warm hand gestures. The kids run around, touching books, looking at toys, sitting on the small rugs dotting the floor. Tyler and I watch them, holding hands, waiting to say good-bye before our flight home later tonight.

As ever, saying good-bye is bittersweet. Renata nearly suffocates me with her hug and swoons when Tyler hugs her too. Big Mom, if I understand correctly, tells me to go home and have my own kids, which makes Tyler chuckle and squeeze my waist. "I'm down with the making part, not sure about the actual outcome for now."

This time too, leaving Raj is a bit harder because the rest of my friends go home to their pleasant lives. Raj stays where pleasant is not the stuff of day-to-day life.

On the plane back, Tyler's plane where the two of us are bundled together on a plush seat, Tyler asks if I'm okay and I tell him all about Raj's hard life. Tyler listens attentively, stroking my hand with his thumb. I go on, unloading my frustration.

"You know, it's so unfortunate that there are so many tragedies out there, but tragedies just like many other things, are measured by numbers. What Raj has seen in his short lifetime — it's heart breaking, Tyler. And what is even more heart breaking is that it takes there being a critical tragedy or someone famous to get the aid moving to the people who need it most. I want that changed." I look up at Tyler, my head on his lap. "It's tragically ridiculous. You know that your haircut made more waves than some of the deadly havoc that happened the same week in some forsaken places around the word?"

Tyler cringes and shakes his head at the absurdity.

"I don't know what I as an individual can do to help besides volunteering," I continue. "But it's clearer to me now than it's ever been before, I want to help those who need help. Maybe make the noise for them. I want to do more, much more. I just need to figure out how."

CHAPTER
Seventeen

Tyler

'm lost in your smell. I'm lost in the way you look at me. I'm lost in your voice whispering in my ears. You light this fire in me. Lyrics swim around in my head as I stare down at Ivi who fell asleep on my lap.

It's such an incredible feeling, having her peacefully sleeping on me. Watching her delicate serene face, I can do this forever. I lightly stroke her silky hair.

Ivi kept on talking, riled up, fired and I've listened attentively though nothing she said was new to me. I know and heard it all before. I know her so well by now, everything about her, but I don't mind her telling me it all over, again and again, because I want to hear her, talking to me, confiding in me. I want to be that person for her.

I know there's something in her that's evolving — a burn. I recognize passion when I see it. But I won't intervene nor attempt to guide her in any way. She needs to figure out what and how she wants to do whatever she wants to do — by herself. I don't want to tell her what to do, I want her it to grow from within her. For her to find her own path, just like I've found mine. Tread through the struggles and hinders and come out wiser. As long as it's by my side, that is. I can't think of an alternative. A future for us together is a future I know will be just right. I can't imagine it any other way. Ivi, Jeremy and me. That's my future, as I see it.

I look out the round window at the endless night sky and inwardly chuckle, thinking about Ivi literally falling on her sweet ass when I finally told I loved her. I should have told her that ages ago, back when I realized she was it for me. That night when she left, when I was lying in my bed struggling to understand what came over me. Trying to figure out how to handle this feeling of losing the best thing that has ever happened to me. At the time, it was like a punch to the gut, the terrifying acknowledgment that I couldn't control whatever was happening, something that if I'm being honest, I wasn't used to.

It's ridiculous how easy it is to sort out most things when you have the means and know the right people. Or hell, just by being famous. At times people will get the fucking moon from the sky for me. The best of everything? You got it. A resident visa for your girlfriend? You got it. But it's the crucial things that you can't control. It's the most important things that can't be fixed by a phone call or a capable manager.

I knew Ivi had strong feelings for me, it wasn't a surprise when she told me she loved me too, but hearing it — Christ, what an overwhelming feeling. Felt like I was on top of the world.

Ivi snuggles closely to me, letting out a sleepy, content sigh. My chest expands with such adoration, I have half a mind to wake her up and kiss her with everything she prompts in me, and more. I check out the time. We still have a couple of hours till we land. I can't wait to see her reaction when she realizes where we're going. I decided to take a detour on our way back, visit Estonia for Ivi to see her parents and friends. A decision that had Eli shitting bricks over the things I have planned for the next week that he'll have to cancel and deal with the consequences of. Fuck that, let him deal, he can manage. My lips tip in amusement. He should be grateful for the quiet time he has had so far concerning me. I've been a damn boy scouts poster boy since Miss Sleepyhead on my lap came along.

Eighteen

"Research has shown that reality shows have an impact on the values of young girls and how they view real – life situations." An article Ivi skimmed through with her morning tea that made her frown with irritation.

"Talk about stress, I've *only* two years to decide on my future, that's insanity," Jeremy says to the wide TV he's currently zoomed in on, titling his body as he presses on the black controller in his hand, making his character load a gun or whatever that was.

Biting on her lip, holding a similar controller, Amelie commands Jeremy, "Left. To the base on the left."

Following Amelie's character, eyes glued to the action on the screen, Jeremy adds, "But no worries I already know what I want to be." His smarty grin blooms. "Of course."

From the sofa by the window, where I'm enthusiastically knitting Jeremy a pair of wooly socks, I ask, "Yeah, Jer, what is it?" Given the jet leg and the physical exertion of the past month, I decided to simply chill upon our return. Maybe it isn't just physical exertion, maybe it's physical exertion with a side of emotional overload. Visiting home was a dream, especially with Tyler, but leaving my parents again was even more difficult than the last time. When I first left it was for a limited time, this time I left with the knowledge that my original home is no longer my home. Both a pleasant and a sad notion.

"Biochemistry and molecular biology." The intonation in which Jeremy tells me his future educational preference sounds like an eye roll where a duh should conclude his answer. Because, of course, what preteen doesn't know with such confidence that biochemistry and molecular biology is his future. "Chase them, Em! They're getting away." Jeremy directs his fellow Fortnight solider.

I tug on the yarn and resume knitting. "What about you, Amelie, any grand plans for the future."

Amelie turns to me with a wide grin.

"Dude — " Jeremy gestures at the screen, "What are you doing?"

Amelie shakes her head, turns back to the game, effortlessly shoots two opponents and turns back to me with that keen smile. "Easy, I want to be you when I grow up."

Startled and pleasantly surprised by her response, I mirror her smile. "Wow, what an honor. What do you mean by that, you want to pursue a volunteering career?"

Amelie lets out a soft chuckle. At this point both kids have left the game and are both turned my way. "No," she giggles. "I want to be as beautiful as you and find me a famous guy like Tyler Lee and be his girlfriend."

The wind? Feels like it's been knocked out of me with a blow of a twenty-pound sledgehammer. "What?" I can't disguise my disappointment, nor the cringe at the thought that this is how she sees me. Not to mention the fact that in one casual statement she managed to bring out of the shadow my greatest fear of Tyler's and my relationship, the fear of losing myself. Wow. Wow, I can't believe this. I'm reeling but try to contain myself before lashing out at the poor girl that has her conception of me entirely twisted. This is how I'm portrayed to people? God.

I set the needles on the end table and readjust to give Amelie my full attention, but before I'm able to thread in a word, Mr. Research Extraordinaire chirps in, "Did you know that being unemployed can be harmful? I read somewhere that it can lead to depression and in some cases even change your personality completely." Jeremy's eyes travel from Amelie to me. He looks a bit uncomfortable seeming to read by my expression that I'm not entirely full of joy. "And it can … " his words fade out. He swallows noticeably, brows wrinkled.

"Listen Amelie, I — " Suddenly, I'm not so sure how to "defend" myself and feminism in general. I'm a little lost for words. Not sure what I can show for myself, really. Somewhat horrifyingly, I can see it clearly now, how I may look from the girl's point of view. I don't have what one might call a "real job." I've left my home and family for a famous guy. She always sees me at home, Tyler's home. I'm a kept woman! I feel a little sick.

"There's much more to life than finding a partner. You need to study. You need to fulfil your dreams. You need to try things and make a mess out of them, then fix them and grow. I may not be officially employed — " another cringe rears its head. "But, up until recently I worked as a nanny, as you know. Other than that, most of my free time and energy had been and still are dedicated to volunteering."

Amelie's smile takes a quizzical quality. "But aren't you in love with Tyler? Aren't you truly happy? You guys are my couple goal."

Couple goal at twelfth? I swear, I feel so old. "I love Tyler, and yes I'm very happy to be in a relationship with him, but that doesn't mean that I don't need anything else besides that." Understatement of the century. "My relationship doesn't define me."

"Amelie honey, your mom is here," Adina calls from the kitchen.

As if we didn't just have a meaningful conversation, and as if she didn't just unpeel a painful wound, and as if she didn't just throw me into an internal self-deprecating loop, cheerfully, Amelie rises to stand.

"See you on Sunday?" She asks Jeremy nonchalantly. Jeremy replies, "Yeah, sure" demonstrating just how close these two best buddies have become, a little after Jeremy stopped drooling every time Amelie breathed.

Nonchalantly she walks over to me and gives me a hug. "I still think that you're the luckiest woman in the world." And off she goes with a carefree gait.

————•————

"You okay, babe?" Tyler whispers to my ear, leaving a soft kiss at my temple.

I nod, indulging in the feel of his strong arms around me. I'm lounged between his legs, facing the rest of the gang scattered on the adjacent couches. I'm having a pleasant time hanging with Tyler's friends, glad to shut off the nagging feeling that's been pestering my thoughts throughout the day. Amelie's words still burned in my mind. Not to mention the snowball of doubts they managed to evoke.

Footsteps coming from the main hall have me avert my attention from Max and Killer's banter. Jay saunters our way in jean overalls and a white Henley. I smile at him.

"Hugsy Wugsy." He taps Tyler's nose with a ridiculing grin. "Missed your cutesy smile."

"Couldn't stop thinking about you all the time I was away, Sugarpuss," Tyler says flatly.

Jay grins at me as I stand to greet him with a hug. "How was visiting home?"

"Perfect," I return.

Killer and Jay do this chin tip men greet thing. "Anyone want anything from the kitchen?" Jay says over his shoulder en route to get a drink.

"Do you think life smokes a cigarette after fucking you up?"

I can't help but shake my head and grin at Max's question.

"What did life ever do to you? Pharmacy out of Xanax?" Killer deadpans.

Max scratches his scruff, grazing his lips with his teeth. "The other day, this chick was going down on m — "

"Dude." Tyler raises his hand in a "spare us please" gesture. "We're good, let's not take it apart right now."

"See," Killer says, nodding a thanks to Jay who just handed him a beer. He returns his attention to Max. "If you were in a relationship you would avoid all this shit." Killer takes a long drag of his bottle. "Grow up, man."

"I can't adult." Max shivers with horror. "This is the real disease of the twenty-first century — giving up the joy of life for the sake of settling down. It's unhealthy and unnatural. Little by little it takes pieces of you. Eats you up."

"That so?" Jay grins. "Glad I'm free as a butterfly." They high five in solidarity.

"Wait till your junk falls off from whatever you catch next," Killer goes on. "Or your tongue."

"I can't believe this is still going on," Tyler says over a sigh.

"Speaking of tongues, anyone tried those Tungdoms?" Max looks around, brows raised as if everyone is ready to sink into a deep conversation about the subject.

By Max's expression I can only guess that Tyler just gave him a reprimanding stare. However, Max immediately recovers and lets out into the air the following pearls of wisdom, "You don't need to worry about your tongue anymore, ah Sir Adams? You got your woman, and it doesn't seem like she's going anywhere."

I'm not even sure how I'm supposed to feel about that.

"Ah, Ivs?" Max turns to me. "You've got a new role in life. Tyler's girl." And he goes on, "Come to think of it, maybe there are some advantages to settling down. You're certainly doing a stellar job of shifting the throngs of wonderful women our way. Way to go Mary Poppins, great job!" Max grins. "Oh, fuck! Can't wait for you to join us on tour! It'll be the bomb to have a mother figure on tour. But I need to warn you, Ivs, don't try to go all momma on me, let me go on my sinful path. Close your eyes when the fangirling wave comes to attack."

I frown. "As truly marvellous as it sounds, I just need to ask, what gave you the impression that I'll be joining you guys on tour?"

"C'mon, almost Mrs. Adams, your destiny was rendered the moment you were claimed by Mr. Adams."

I gape at him. *What's going on with people today?* And a beat later, I lash out. "First off, when we get married, I won't change my name!" Realising what flew out of my mouth in the heat of the moment, my face catches on fire. Sometimes I wish the things that came out of my mouth were a little more intellectually sensible. "I mean." I gulp. "Not that I'm under any assumption, or considering, us, umm … I — I just wanted to state a point." I couldn't be more grateful for not being able to meet Tyler's eyes. Tyler, who'd stiffened behind me. Opting to stir away from the matrimonial elephant I just dropped in the middle of the room, I say, "Max, you know I do have a life besides hanging with you guys, right?"

"He's just being his usual dumbass self," Tyler causally says, seeming, or pretending to not take issue with my verbal diarrhoea or the subject that's about to make me explode.

Max reads something on his phone, grins widely like he's found a treasure and rises to his feet. His grin grows as he towers over me, peeking again at his phone, as if reading a script. "Repeat after me," he tells me next, another glance at the phone. "I, beautiful miss Ivi Kert, do solemnly swear and pledge my sword to Tyler Lee Adams and his band as my liege, to defend and obey them until they depart their demesnes or death shall take me, and to uphold the honor of groupiehood."

Concluding this nonsense, he stretches his arm to mimic a sword as he hovers it over my shoulder and head. Tyler, finding it amusing, chuckles lightly. Jay follows suit. Max, utterly pleased with himself, declares, "Arise, Miss Groupie Number One."

"Okay enough, cut this shit, Max," Tyler says still utterly amused.

Any other day, I might have cracked a smile or even joined the hilarity, but not today. Today all I want to do is give him a piece of my mind, or punch him. But I don't. What good would it do to scold him? It would only prove that I am Mary Poppins after all.

CHAPTER
Nineteen

" ... *the study suggests these results go hand-in-hand: women are more likely to see their careers and personal welfare take a backseat to those of their partners." The morning news blaring along to the sound of a boiling kettle.*

Tyler's girlfriend. Tyler's house. Tyler's friends. Tyler's kid. Tyler's tempo. Where is *Ivi* in all of this?

"Here you go, dear," Adina says in a gentle voice, handing me fresh toast together with a concerned glance. She stealthily makes herself scarce right after.

My blank stare falls on my untouched cup of coffee; a whole moment passes till I realize that the toast I've dropped in the toaster some time ago is now lying on a plate blackened. I was so caught up in my own head that I didn't even noticed Adina remove the burned slice and toast a new one for me. Snippets of last night keep flashing in my mind like a fast-paced movie. *"Find me a famous person like Tyler and be his stay at home girlfriend."* The little chat with Amelie that started it off. *"You've got a new role in life. Tyler's girl."* Max adding the last drop of fuel to bring the fire burning in me to a monstrous blaze. Excusing myself early. Pretending to fall asleep when Tyler got into bed, a task that got harder when he spooned me and gently kissed my head. Getting up to call Chris when I couldn't lay there anymore with the conflicting emotions battling in my gut. How Tyler's soft breathing as I got out of bed lit my determination to do something about it.

"Chris, remember that job you mentioned the last time we spoke, something about a coordinator for YWPO?"

"Yeah, a project coordinator. Funny you should mention it. I've been meaning to talk to you about it. You still interested?"

"Yes." I couldn't have sounded more resolved.

"We're looking to man the position in a few weeks. As it happens, the management is meeting in Vegas next Tuesday. Do you think you could make it? You know, it's better to have everyone interviewing, meeting you in person at the same time than video call interviews and the headache of coordinating it all."

"Sure. I can do that."

"I'll email you the details later today." There's a pause. *"I thought your relationship was going well. You just came back from Nepal. It was all over the media."* He clears his throat. *"Sure you're ready to leave?"*

"It's going well." This time my words come out a bit less determined.

"Good to hear." There's clearly still an unanswered question hanging in the air, but Chris doesn't probe any further. A gesture that on the one hand is welcomed and appreciated, but on the other, perhaps I should have consulted with someone, or just vented out what's been bothering me. But it feels a bit unfair to do it with Chris when the person I should be discussing it with is Tyler.

That was last night. That, and then there was my foolish avoidance of Tyler. Not that he did anything wrong, it was just me being a complete coward. Too hesitant to broach my fresh decision with him. That eventually led to a sleepless night and a morning full of uncertainties.

Spreading butter on my toast, I try to explore what I'm really feeling. It was a concern of mine right from the moment I knew I was coming back, the ambiguity of what I was coming back to, besides Tyler. I couldn't be more sure about how much I love him and want to be with him. There's zero doubt there. But I'm not less convinced that I need to find my thing — apart from him. Something for myself. I never even entertained the idea of not doing something with myself. Something valuable and meaningful. Something that would fulfil me. Nor did I ever plan to lose myself in a man. In a way, I feel like I'm walking around in constant yellow warning, like something will happen and I might lose it all, the things I have and the ones I don't, yet.

By the time evening falls and Tyler enters the living room's threshold, I'm determined to go ahead with my plan. Time to woman up and do the right thing. Communicate. The real true essence of any healthy relationship is communication. Okay, communication and sex.

"Hey you," I give him a genuine smile, because no matter what's troubling me, every time we're apart I miss him.

Tyler's lips stretch into a glorious smile. He doesn't greet me back, instead he closes the distance between us quicker than I can say *God you look delicious* and lifts me into a kiss-hug duo of awesome proportions. A greeting that has me panting a little.

"Fucking missed you," he says, leaving my lips only to nuzzle my collarbone. "Coming home to you is the best part of my day."

I swallow hard with the message I'm about to deliver sitting like lead in my stomach. Then, almost artfully, Tyler makes me forget my resolve with his lips on my skin and his hard body against mine. "Adina's left?" He rasps while sliding his hand into the back of my jeans.

"Ye—s," comes out breathy. So are my next words as Tyler drops us onto the nearest couch and drops to his knees. A beat later, I'm freed of my pants. A moan later, my panties are shoved to the side and I gasp. Everything fades away. I want to watch. I want to see the magnificent vision of Tyler's concentrated, heated face as he gives me pleasure. I lean on my elbows and drink him up with my eyes. Fire travels along the length of my skin. I am throbbing with an almost painful, delightful sensation. I'm panting and trembling, it's nearly too wonderfully much. I quiver, dropping my head back, my eyes tightly shut as I cry out his name. I'm thankful we're alone in the house because I'm pretty sure my chants of ecstasy can be heard through the roof. I fall apart only to reach so high again when Tyler thrusts into me and chases his own release.

It feels so incredibly intimate and right to have dinner together in our post sex bliss. I face Tyler, sitting on the floor in his discarded Nirvana Tee and woolly, stripy green and orange socks up to my knees. Tyler is in boxers, his bare body a feast to my eyes. I sip on Tom Yam from a mug with my legs bent, toes dug under Tyler's thigh, while he feeds me Pad Thai with chopsticks in-between his own mouthfuls.

Tyler swallows and tips his chin at the mug in my hands. With a soft smile, I tilt forward to bring the mug to his lips. He rewards me with a thin grin of gratitude. "I need to be in New York on Monday, wanna join me? We can stay for a couple of nights, make a short getaway out of it."

"Umm, I can't, I'll need to be in Vegas on Monday." I lower my gaze, taking great interest in the mug in my hands.

Tyler's brows wrinkle. "Vegas?" He brings another load of noodles to his mouth.

"Yes, there's this thing I've been meaning to tell you about right when you came back but got a little side-tracked." I lift my stare to his.

"Really?" Tyler's eyes sparkle with mirth. "What is it, Kiis?"

I set the mug on the low table and hug my knees. "I spoke to Chris last night." Tyler splits his attention between the steaming bowl in his hand and me. "He mentioned that a job he thought I'd be interested in became available and asked me to fly out to Vegas for interviews with the YWOP management."

Tyler mounts another load on the chopsticks. "What position are they talking about?"

"A project coordinator," I say and then swiftly add in a lower tone, "Based out of Texas — what do you say, exciting, ah?"

Tyler's eyes lift to me, the chopsticks suspended in mid-air. "It's in Texas?"

"Yes, that's where the offices are based. So, what do you say?" I opt to maintain a light tone.

Tyler stabs the sticks in the diminishing pile of noodles. "Will you be traveling there often?" He wipes his mouth with a napkin. "Is it something you can do remotely?"

I shake my head.

Tyler places the bowl of food and the crumbled napkin on the table, a little too aggressively. A strange feeling winds up in my chest, like we're going to fight. Like I'm going to get hurt and disappointed. "What do I say?" He says to the bowl with an incredulous chuckle. He turns to me. "It's a couple thousand miles away." He cocks his head, studying me, his jaw tight. "And you want to take it?"

I nod again, finding it hard to hold a neutral expression.

"I don't get it," he says seeming utterly startled. "Wasn't the point of you coming back for us to be together?" He slightly shakes his head in bewilderment. "I don't get it." His eyes hard on mine. "Did we come so far just for you to go away?"

I tighten my embrace on my bent legs. "Tyler, it's a bit unfair and sort of selfish for you to say that. I have a shot at a career and, you know — it's my life."

"And what, Ivi?" His frown deepens. "I'm being selfish for wanting my girlfriend next to me? For us to be together? When will we see each other exactly, with my traveling and you three states away?" He scratches his scruff absently.

"We can make long distance work," I say determined.

He retorts, "Can we?" Tyler's mouth twists. "Selfish," he repeats to the room on a sigh. Turning to look at me again, he adds, "You know what? *I am* selfish when it comes to you. I want you, all the time. I want you near me. I'm not going to apologize for that." He pauses. "Ivi, do you understand that we'll hardly see each other, that's what you want?"

I take a deep breath, my next words coming out harsher and quicker. "My life basically revolves around you. I have nothing for myself here. If I want to make roots here, they should be mine. God, Tyler, I'm the very definition of a kept woman." I want to retch at the thought. "I live in *your* house. Eat *your* food. Hang out with *your* friends. It's as if nothing is really mine in this relationship."

"I'm yours," Tyler's stare locks on mine. "I thought that was enough," he adds under his breath. He takes my hand in his. "You want me to call my lawyer and sign the house over to you? I can arrange it immediately."

My eyes grow in surprise. "What? No!" Comes out as a shocked exhalation. "You don't get it, do you?" I drop my hand from his. Looking at him in dismayed irritation I say, "Tyler, you're so off track here. It's not about property or anything materialistic. It's about me wanting to fulfil my desires and us being equal which to me seems like it's almost impossible. You are who you are, you can't change that. I don't want you to change but in the same breath I want to do something for me, to grow as an individual." I hold his stare. "A name on a deed won't do that."

Tyler is quiet for some stretched moments. He leans to rest his arms on his thighs, his fingers steepled together. He looks ahead as he talks, "I don't have my hand anywhere near the emergency brake when it comes to us. I try to embrace whatever comes our way because I'm in for the long haul." He cranes his neck to give me a sidelong look. "Is this really your dream job? Is it worth putting us on the backburner?" His stare at me deepens. "To me it sounds a bit like an escape plan because things are getting serious."

Escape plan. Is it some sort of an escape plan? I bite on my lips because suddenly they start to tremble. "Tyler, don't do that. That's unfair. I'm not choosing anything over you and you know that. I'm just — "

Tyler rises to stand, folding his arms across his chest, looking frustrated. "You know what? Do whatever you want. You're not going to listen to me anyway. From where I'm standing, it looks like you've made up your mind long before talking to me." He spreads his arms in defeated frustration. "With that said," he stares me down. "You know what, Ivi? When you find someone you see a future with, you try to learn how to make your rhythms synch. Try to see how you can incorporate your wills, so you stay true to yourself, but not at the cost of being together. I'd do anything to make you happy, Ivi. And above all, I want us to work. You living in a different state and me traveling most of the time, not to mention *I have a kid in LA* — I can't follow you." He shakes his head somewhat exasperated. "I want Jeremy to be a constant in my life, just as I want you to be one. People adjust and make it work when they really want it to work." He shrugs in defeat. "Maybe I was wrong. Maybe I'm not that person for you, but just to make it clear, sure as hell you're *that* person for me."

"Tyler." I stand up.

"What, Ivi, what?" he raises his voice. When I don't reply, as I'm too confused to even form an intelligent response, Tyler says, "I'm gonna — " He tips his head in the direction of the recording studio.

With a bitter forlorn smile, I ask, "You need some space?"

Tyler blinks swiftly, asserting that, yes, he needs some space… away from me.

And I'm left alone. Completely bare and shivering underneath his shirt, I note that I still smell of him. It makes the moment that much harder to bear.

After an hour that seem like an eternity, I go up to the bedroom, not surprised yet disappointed, that he doesn't come up to seek me. I toss and turn till the wee hours of the night by myself in bed and fall asleep *alone*.

CHAPTER
Twenty

CHAPTER

"I wish someone would talk about me the way Tyler Lee talks about Ivi. That last interview for the @rollingstone, sisters! I died all dies!"
A tweet by @TherealMrsAdams tagging @TylerLeeAdams and @IviK

9:00 a.m.

The day begins like any other day, any other day with a stomach laden with unease and minus one boyfriend. Tyler is nowhere to be seen when I finally manage to peel myself out of bed. I feel like I have a hangover even though not a drop of alcohol touched my lips last night. I shower quickly and shrug on a pair of boyfriend jeans and a large, black off the shoulder shirt. I don't bother with makeup, puffy eyes or not. I'm definitely not in the mood for fussing over my looks.

9:25 a.m.

I futilely look for Tyler around the house and contemplate for a long moment whether to call him or not. Disturbed and disappointed by the fact that this is the way he chose to handle our disagreement, or whatever it was, I decide to not call him. Two can play this dumb power game. Instead, I bring up the Uber app and order a ride to a little coffee shop I frequent regularly, less than inclined to stay at home and stew over this.. A change of scenery is not a bad idea. Especially if said change of scenery involves people gazing and a tea.

10:00 a.m.

A steaming chai latte is cradled between my hands as I gaze out the window, taking in the busy world outside. People going about their day, pleased with an agenda, with a purpose. It's hard to wrap my head around what I'm feeling right now. It's a cauldron of opposing emotions. There's anger, sadness, frustration, compassion and understanding, all boiling in me. Tyler's justifications toward the end of our argument were legitimate and made lots of sense. He can't follow me. His entire life is based in L.A. with Jeremy as the crux of his reluctance to even consider the idea of moving away. That's something I'd never want him to change for me. Not to mention, we both know full-well that this isn't about a dream job. Not even close. With that said, right from the start he was too vocal about his displeasure of the idea of me moving away. He didn't really listen to what I was saying or try to come up with a solution together. To him, my moving away is a death sentence to our relationship. Is it? He didn't even offer to try it out for a while, try to make long-distance work. Thinking about it, out of all the emotions, anger seems to lead the race at this point. That fuels and nurtures my thoughts to grow with irritation. A small voice peeps through the resentment, *it was all about him not wanting to lose you.* The downside to this comforting notion is that the way he delivered it was immensely selfish and inconsiderate.

10:15 a.m.

I haven't touched my chai. Yes, my mind is spinning. Yes, I am mad. Yes, it's absurdly ridicules not to talk things out. Yes, this wedge between us is tearing me at the seams. I don't believe in wars, I believe in peace, negotiations and a happier world. Maybe it's time to offer an olive branch. I pull out my phone and set it on the table in front of me, mentally preparing to make the call.

10:20 a.m.

Five minutes of staring at an inanimate device is enough to make it a touch ludicrous. That's it, I'm not sure what I'm going to say, all I know is that I need to say something, and it has to be said right now. I pick up the phone, my heart is banging in my chest and … it startles me with a chime. I jerk back a little, surprised by the unexpected development. The phone rings again with Tyler's name at the bottom of the image of his beautiful face flashing at me. My emotions are all over the place when I answer with a subdued, "Hey."

"Ivi," Tyler's voice alone makes me stiffen in my seat. A pause. "Jeremy and Melena are in the hospital."

My hand flies to my mouth, all the prior bedlam erased by one short sentence. "What? Are they okay, what happened?"

"No." Another pause, a chilling one. "There was an accident, we're at Cedars–Sinai."

"I'm coming."

10:29 a.m.

My head is throbbing; my lips are about to bleed from the assault of my teeth. I look out the window, but I see nothing. Typical L.A. is traffic and the Uber slowly crawls. Too slow. The navigation system shows a twenty minute estimated time of arrival. I'm a tight spring of apprehension as I inwardly urge the cars in fronts of us to move faster. The song on the radio is followed by a news feed. Only fragments of information really sink in, congressman, assault, shooting, Brexit across the pond. Abruptly, my ears perk up. "What did they just say?" I ask the driver.

He glances at me via the rear-view mirror. "That singer's Tyler

Lee Adams, his son was in a car accident. They said he's in critical condition." He shakes his head. "Crazy world we're living in, ah?"

10:35 a.m.

I feel like a massive quake just hit me, leaving me with my feet at either side of the crack where I'm not sure which side to take but know full-well that not taking a side isn't an option. My heart stops for a breath and when it beats again, it hurts. *Critical condition.* The Uber app shows about half a mile to go which seems like it'll take forever in this heavy traffic. "Can you pull over?"

"Ma'am, were not there yet."

"Please pull over." It's a plea.

10:36 a.m.

The car doesn't even come to a complete stop as I jump out. I'm still able to hear the reprimanding "miss" the driver calls out as I start running toward the hospital like my life depended on it, all the while holding back tears of panic that are threatening to break free any minute.

10:46 a.m.

Jogging through the sliding doors to the ER, my eyes run everywhere, searching, not sure for what. Spotting the information desk, I dash over, my words stumble on one another at the nurse behind the counter, "Jeremy Adams, he's here. I mean, Jeremy Nathan Brown. He's supposed to be here."

The nurse doesn't even look Jeremy up in the records before muttering, "You'll have to go through that guy." She tips her head at a tall guy in a dark suit. I briskly walk over to the guy in subject which I quickly realise must be a security personal. Word already got out, people know that Tyler is here. For a moment I feel sorry for Tyler, even his most private moments are public, and there's nothing he can do about it. "I'm Ivi — Tyler's … " I stammer, pleading at the guy in the suit.

He nods at me mid-sentence. "Room number five, down that hall." A meaty finger points behind his shoulder.

10:51 a.m.

"Ben." Ben, who's standing by door number five gives me a consolation smile, tipping his chin in greeting. He takes a step forward to open the door to allow me in. I step in to a bland waiting room with a sofa and a low table, whitewashed walls and Tyler sitting on a plastic chair. He's leaning forward, elbows on his knees, his face ashen. I stand by the door, the lump in my throat making it hard to speak. Tylor's shattered eyes capture mine. I take a few steps to stand before him, my expression mirroring his. His Adam apple descends as he swallows, perhaps pushing down his own fears. Wordlessly, he sends his hand to grab a fistful of my shirt. Tyler pulls me closer to him and buries his face in my stomach. I'm choked up on emotions and worries as I wrap my hands around his head, leaning down to put my lips to the crown of his head.

We stay still for some stretched, silent moments, holding on to each other, too staggered to form words. We break apart only when Eli enters the room, moments later, stone-faced, carrying a travel tray with hot beverages.

I turn to bring a chair to sit next to Tyler, but he halts me by pulling at my hand. I turn back to him in question. Tyler wraps his arm around my waist and gently sits me on his lap. An act of dependence, of needing me, to hold on to. His arm stays around my waist as he accepts a hot drink from Eli.

"Ivi?" Eli offers me one too.

I shake my head. "Thanks, I'm good."

"Any update?" Eli asks, pulling out a stick of gum from a pack in his pocket.

"Nothing," Tyler says on an exhale.

Eli nods, chewing on the gum. "I'm going to see if I can get anything." He walks out of the room.

"What happened?" I finally ask Tyler in a quiet voice. "Where's Jeremy?"

Tyler's features harden in agony. "Some paparazzi followed their car. Melena got distracted and they say she lost control of the car and hit a tree."

I gasp.

"The airbags were deployed but Melena has a fractured forearm and a concussion. She's pretty bruised up." Tyler swallows, seeming to have a hard time letting out his next words. "Jeremy," he says and clears his throat. "They're still checking him, they suspect a head injury. Question is how serious it is."

I watch Tyler with a hand over my mouth. A knock on the door has us turn our attention to the front of the room. Two doctors in white coats enter the room, the older one with wire-framed glasses and a clipboard, says, "Mr. Adams." The other, a younger man with his mask hanging at his neck follows his senior colleague.

Tyler stands, and so do I. The older surgeon extends his hand for a shake, "I'm Dr. Soames, and this is Dr. Nicholas." We shake both men's hands.

The younger Dr. Nicholas, says, "We'd like to give you an update," squinting my way.

Tyler follows his gaze. "Go ahead, Ivi's family."

I take Tyler's hand in mine, to support him. To support myself.

Dr. Soames leafs through the clipboard and straightens his stare. "Your son was moved to intensive care. He suffered a trauma to the head from the airbag. There was some swelling and localized bleeding in the surrounding tissues." Pause. "We induced a coma to give time for the swelling to go down."

Tyler's hand weakens in mine and I squeeze gently, wordlessly reminding him that I'm here for him.

"Coma?" Tyler clears his throat, his voice still comes out gravelly as he asks, "For how long? What's next? Is there any damage?"

"We'll wait to see if the swelling recedes and go from there. I can't give you a timeframe right now, it depends on the brain's healing pace."

"Do you expect any after effects?" I ask in a cautious tone.

"It's hard to know at the moment, we're dealing with a severe situation. It's really hard to say if there'll be any effects later on. We need to just take it one step at a time."

Tyler's features are tight with pain, the muscle above his eyes working as he takes a deep breath. "Thank you."

"Mr. Adams I know it's hard to wait for answers, but please know we have him monitored by our best people. I assure you, we are giving him the best treatment possible."

Tyler nods somewhat mechanically. "When can we see him?"

"We'll let you know as soon as possible."

When the doctors leave the room, Tyler covers his eyes with his hands, he slides them higher, holding his head and shakes it lightly in utter bewilderment. "Fuck, fuck, fuck."

"Tyler," I slide my hand to his waist. "Tyler."

Keeping his bemused, agonized pose, he murmurs to himself. "This is all me."

My gaze darts up to him. "What?"

"He's here, fighting for his life because of me."

"What? No! Don't say that."

"It's true." Determined. "They were after them because of me, because he is my son. This would have never happened if I'd just let it be, let him live a normal life. Not be chased by fucking photographers. Why did I have to do that? I should have never brought him into this to begin with."

I take a step to stand before him. "Tyler, look at me." I wait for his eyes to meet mine. "Tyler, Jeremy loves you. He adores you. He looks up to you. He couldn't be prouder being your child. Knowing you. I'm sure he wouldn't change it for the world." Tyler looks entirely tortured and it breaks my heart. I lean forward and wrap my arms around his waist and press my cheek to the center of his chest. I say nothing, because it feels like no matter what I say it won't take his guilty feelings away.

Holding Tyler, with all my heart I pray this experience will end up family lore and not something that'll impact Jeremy for life, or worse.

CHAPTER
Twenty-one

"Finally, it's quiet."
"I prefer the chaos. The noise is so much better, silence scares me."
A conversation between two nurses at the front station.

The scene is hard to take in. In a way, it feels surreal. It's not gruesome, or heinous, on the contrary, it's clean and quiet. Too clean and quiet. Too clinically clean and frighteningly still.

Tyler clasps my hand so tight it pulsates. I can feel his tension flow through to me while absorbing my own anxiety in return. The room is a standard hospital room with its sterile aesthetics. Florescent light, pale walls. The machines and tubes intimidating, but what makes the scene petrifying to me is the preteen that looks so small and frail, lying still in the vast bed. Energetic, goofy, smiling, adorable Jeremy is pale, almost as bleached as the sheets he lies on. The kid lying on the bed looks like a faded carbon copy of the boisterous boy whose been residing in my heart since the first time I met him. An automatic ventilator sticking out of his mouth forces Jeremy's chest to rise and fall in rhythm to its mechanically daunting, steady noise.

Tyler clears his throat, it sounds like a strangled choke. We stand still by the bed, looking at Jeremy incomprehensibly. Tyler's hand leaves mine as he bends in half to place a gentle kiss in the center of his son's forehead. He takes a step back to stand next to me, tall and broad and utterly shuddering. "You know, he always has this little, faint crooked smile on." His eyes trained on his son. "Even when he sleeps."

My own lips lift a little in sentiment. "Yes." Is a soft whisper. "He has the most beautiful smile." *All I want is to see it again.*

Tyler inhales heavily and shakes his head. He scrubs his hand over his stubble. "Why," he breathes on an exhale. "Why him?"

I lean closer, resting my head on Tyler's shoulder. Seems like ages pass as we stand, just stand, trying to understand, trying to make sense of this dreadful reality.

Somewhere between Eli bringing us food that neither of us can even look at to Jay stopping by, I fall asleep on the armchair by Jeremy's bed.

Soft caresses on my hair stir me from a troubled sleep. I gently flicker my eyes open to a softly lit room. Night greets me from the large windows as I scan the room. Feels like I dozed for a few hours.

"Hey," Tyler's voice comes from close behind me, just next to my ear. That's when I realize I'm nestled in his arms on the same armchair I fell asleep in. At a certain point Tyler must have lifted me up only to take me in his arms. I crane my neck to look at him and stretch just a little to press a kiss to the corner of his mouth.

Tyler offers me a bottle of water from the table. I take a long drink and give it back to him. He looks at me for a stretched moment. "I'm sorry for my outburst yesterday," he says in a low voice.

I take his hand in mine, threading our fingers and mirror his soft tone. "It really doesn't matter right now."

Eyes still deep into mine he resumes. "No, it *is* important. Better say what's on your heart and not wait till it's too late." The soft light in the room makes his eyes shine. They shift to Jeremy before returning to mine. "When I came back home last night, I had a completely different end to the night in mind. I bought you something and I wanted to give it to you, but then we got distracted and later you had that news for me, and I sort of lost it a little. I'm sorry. I'm not saying I'm okay with it, I just wanted to say that I should have handled it differently."

"Tyler, about that."

Tyler shakes his head, communicating, "It doesn't matter." I take his hand in mine. "I agree, yes we didn't handle it well. Both of us. I should have talked to you before making my own decision about my future."

"Our future." Comes as a resolute emphasis.

"Our future. I understand where you were coming from, I do. I just, well, for us to work, I need something for myself. I wouldn't feel complete without fulfilling my own goals."

"I'd never hold you back from pursuing your dreams, Ivi. I just hope your plans include me."

I nod pensively. "They do, Tyler. They include you both." I pivot to look at Jeremy.

Tyler sends his hand to gently pull me toward him. For a frail moment, before leaving a chaste, sweet kiss on my lips, he holds my stare intently. "Go to that meeting on Monday, hear what they have to say first, come back home and we'll go from there."

I nod twice, processing.

"Now, about yesterday." Tyler's teeth graze his lips. "When I came home, there was something I wanted to give you." He looks a bit apprehensive digging into his front pocket. Tyler produces a small, velvet box.

I squint at the box. My breath traps somewhere in my ribcage. It's the kind of box that usually kicks off a couples' unified life-journey.

Tyler's eyes lift to mine and drop back to the box in his hand, mine follow suit. He opens the box to reveal a delicate, gold necklace with a guitar pick charm with "Tyler Lee" carved in the center.

I glance up at him. "It's beautiful. I love it."

Tyler holds the box in an open palm, stare on mine. "Last night, I wanted to give you my first name," he swallows, not breaking our stare. "Till you chose to take my last."

My lips part in awe. I'm lost for words. One way or another, Tyler just made the greatest promise to me. My eyes run over his handsome features. "Tyler."

"Turn your head." I do as told. He gently brushes my hair to one side and secures the necklace around my neck.

I dip my chin to look at the little toggle with Tyler's name decorating my neckline. I brush it with my fingertips. Tyler's look at me is almost tangible. I lift my eyes into his and what transpires has my next breath catch in my chest.

Sometimes, the bravest, strongest, most meaningful things are said in silence.

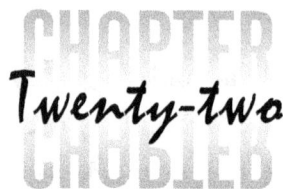

Twenty-two

Waiting Room

*- A sign in the hospital Ivi has been gazing at with absorbed attention,
contemplating how apt it is to her current state.*

Tyler's brows pinch, his stance rigid as he nods at Dr. Soames. He folds his arms across his chest. From where I'm sitting, talking on the phone with Chris as he gives me some final details regarding my Vegas trip, I manage to hear the gist of their conversation.

"Propofol," says Dr. Soames as he briefs Tyler. "Some fully recover and are completely unaffected by the coma. Others may suffer from disabilities caused by the damage to their brain." He listens to what Tyler tells him next. He nods. "It's impossible to accurately predict, sir. It depends on the severity of the damage to the brain, the patient age and how long they've been in a coma. Once he's conscious and responsive we'll run some tests to assess his condition."

"How long before he wakes?" Tyler says.

"It depends on the patient; it could be within minutes or hours after the effect has been ceased."

Tyler nods. Somewhat startled by Chris's voice, I'm pulled back to our conversation. "Let me know if anything changes." Chris concludes our short call. "Hang in there, kid. Hope to hear some good news soon."

"I will. Thanks again. I'll let you know."

When I tuck my phone back in my pocket and turn to look at Tyler, I catch him brushing Jeremy's hair off his forehead. The way Tyler looks at Jeremy, the tenderness in which he tends to his son makes me fall even deeper in love with him.

A nock on the door has us both shift our attention to where Melena is standing, some bruises decorating her face, her arm in a sling but otherwise she appears to have come out of the car wreck nearly unscathed.

Tyler walks over to her, meeting her in a half hug. "You look much better."

"I'm fine. I just talked to the doctors." She glances at Jeremy. "They say he should be waking up soon."

Rubbing Melena's arm, Tyler says emphatically, "It can take a bit longer than that, we have to be patient."

Tyler and I leave the room, allowing Melena some privacy with her son.

Stirring a cup of lacklustre hospital coffee, Tyler asks me, "About what you said earlier about skipping the meeting, I think you should go on Monday, at least hear what they're offering. Melena and I are here with him, it's fine, really." Tyler hands me the coffee and inserts additional coins into the machine.

"I don't think I'll take it," I muse out loud.

He glances at me over his shoulder. Retrieving a steaming cup, he stares at it. "Why?"

"It's just a job, not anywhere my dream job. And mainly because I don't want to leave you. Both of you."

Tyler nods. "Okay, and what do you want to do, if you had your choice, no limitations whatsoever." He leans on the wall behind him, attention trained on me.

I blow on the coffee and take a sip. "Mainly what I've been doing so far as a volunteer, but maybe on a greater scale. Help people, tell their story, make their voices heard. But I don't think I have the power to do that, just me. It'll probably have to be through some organization but getting an actual paying job in these places is a long shot."

"Just because you can't reach a lot of people doesn't mean that you don't have the same impact on the people you're reaching." Tyler says. "You've already been doing it." He pauses. "Kiis," and then, "you know that you don't have to worry about money, right?"

I shake my head. "It won't work this way. I can't and I won't be dependent on you, Tyler."

"Tyler," Melena's raised, labored voice breaks our intent stare down. "Tyler, he's awake."

Twenty-Three

CHAPTER
CHAPTER

*"Wherever you may be in the world, actions speak louder
than words and we acknowledge that."*
*The hotel infomercial playing on the TV while Ivi lies on the bed,
staring at the ceiling.*

Jay: You're welcome ☺.

glance at Jay's odd message. Trying to be stealth so the people
discussing the next YWOP projects around me won't notice, I check
my phone's screen for the image that follows said cryptic text. A warm
smile blossoms on my lips to the image of Jeremy faintly smiling at the
camera, his hand captured is a wave. In the picture, Tyler is squeezed
by Jeremy's side, sound asleep, his big tattooed hand holding his son's.
I love them both, I do. I'd do anything for them. And the last thing I
really want to do is put distance between us.

"Ivi," Chris addresses me. I tuck my phone away, focusing my
attention on him. He leans closer, lowering his voice. "What do you
say, then?" Meaning to ask if I'd like to take the job.

"I'm grateful for the opportunity." I take a sip of water. "Also, it's a
great opportunity to get to know the organization better."

"But?" He prompts.

"I think I want to do more. This job is more administrative. I'd like to be a part of the team that does the field work rather than run it from an office." Also, I don't think that I'm ready to relocate now, or ever, but I keep that to myself.

Chris nods. "Understood."

"If it's possible, I'd like to help you guys from remote until you find the right person for the job."

"I'll run it by the others and let you know. Appreciate it."

———— ◆ ————

"Will that be all, miss?" Says the room service guy while a tad mockingly eyeing the rich offering I've ordered for dinner. With his judgemental smirk he extinguishes my prior thought of ordering a sundae for later. Even though he managed to get me a tad irked, I still tip him. I'm just that kind of person.

His grin together with his cadence morphs flirty. "Dinning solo tonight?"

I cinch my robe tighter. "None of your business," I snap and promptly regret being rude, immediately giving him another note just before walking forward, urging him to leave my room. At the tap of the door closing, I pile my hair high on my head and tie it with an elastic band. Not entirely sure what to make of what I'm feeling, I drop to the bed. If I knew better, I'd say I'm about to get my period, but it's not that. I feel a bit emotional. Maybe a little more than just a bit. Hence the wealth of comfort food teasing me from the silver platter. Let's just say there are enough calories on that platter to properly feed a nuclear family … and their pet. Which instantly makes me feel awful. Such a waste! I don't really need all this. Yes, emotional state is off the rails.

Placing the loot on the bed, I pull back the sleeves of the two sizes too big bathrobe and grab the burger. I bite into the bun and as I chew my eyes well up. When I swallow, somewhat hard, the damn dam breaks and tears roll down my face like it's a slip and slide party. I've clearly hugely underestimated my vulnerability. It's a given, when so many things happen to you in a short time and you hold them all in, keeping your cool, trying to stay intact for too long. Eventually you'll crack. I look at the juicy burger through a glossy screen, whipping my eyes on the oversized sleeves. And everything, *everything,* that was bottled up, till the very last drop, gushes out. I'm sitting on the bed in some estranged hotel with Sin City's colourful lights flickering through the vast windows, sobbing my heart out. With my toes I push away the little jewellery box and the piece of paper I absentmindedly scribbled on earlier as if they are the enemy.

I feel like I belong and not at the same time. Amelie's words. Max's words. Arguing with Tyler. Petrified of losing Jeremy. Jeremy lying in a hospital bed hooked to a ventilator. Tyler giving me that charm with his name and a promise. Leaving them both to go to Vegas. And *the engagement ring* I bought Tyler earlier today! Everything that's swirling in my head reduces me to a messy pile of erratic emotions bawling into a pillow, in Vegas! Definitely hormones going wacko. Through the sounds of my meltdown I manage to hear the chime of my phone. Grabbing the device, I am met with an image of Tyler's smiling face which only intensifies the stream of tears rolling down my face. I choke a sob and answer. "Hey."

"Kiisu?"

I swallow, trying to compose myself.

"Ivi, you okay?" Tyler asks over my pause.

"Ye — s." I sniff. "Sure, how's — " sniff. "Jer." Sniff. "Mi?"

"What's wrong?" Tyler's voice is an octave, or two, tenser. "Ivi?"

I really try to tone it down by taking a deep breath but the only thing that comes out is a strangled sob.

"Ivi, you need to talk to me, baby. I need to know what's going on."

How do I put into words that my heart utterly burns for him? That all I want in this world right now is him. "I miss you." I wipe my tears with the pillow. "I miss you so much right now. I don't know what's come over me, but — " I need to take another breath since oxygen seem to be scarce in the room.

"What's going on, did anything happen to you? Talk to me, Kiisu."

I shake my head even though he can't really see me. "No ... I — just. I don't know. Everything. I just feel a bit emotional."

"A bit?" Tyler asks, his tone an octave lighter.

I exhale a teary laugh. "Talk about making your boyfriend run for the hills."

Tyler's chuckle makes the tight ring in my stomach loosen some. "The last thing your boyfriend wants to do is run for the hills." His humours lilt lingers over the brief pause. "Maybe just drop by the nearest pharmacy for some, umm, Rescue Remedy?"

"Ha. Tell you what?" I manage to stop the waterfall. "Maybe just shift delete everything you heard till now from your memory. I'm just being silly."

Tyler drops the banter and asks, "Remind me, when's your flight back?"

"The only available flight was for tomorrow evening." I take a deep breath, shake my head lightly, still trying to make sense of my behavior, I whisper, "I don't know what is it about tonight, but I miss you so much, Tyler."

"Miss you too, Kiis."

After persuading Tyler that my unbalanced outburst is a product of exhaustion, he finally lets me end our call with a promise to call him at any time if I need to talk. I collect my untouched feast and set it on the table, once again feeling horrible about the waste. I put the box and the paper on the nightstand and enter the bathroom. I wash my face, brush my teeth and change from the robe to Tyler's, #JBiebs have my baby, T-shirt and dive under the covers.

It's too early to sleep so no matter how long I try, I can't bring myself to keep my eyes shut for more than a few minutes. Not to mention the myriad of thoughts filling my mind to the brim that keep me troubled. I scrutinize choices I've made recently. Choices. Life, it is all about choices. Every single moment, unconsciously, or not, we have to make a choice. Our choices lead us to greatness, self-fulfilment, to being a better human, or more than often, not. By a fleet decision you can become someone's hero, or beacon your own demise. Long ago I took an oath, one where I pledged to always consider others, always try to be a better person, because no matter what you do or how you feel, you can always make someone a little happier.

Slowly but surely ideas pop into my head, signalling the path to what I want to do next, career-wise. And it feels reassuring. Feeling a bit more relaxed, I start sensing the heaviness of slumber weighing on me, soothing my body to sink deeper into the mattress. I yawn, snuggling deeper underneath the downy comforter and my eyes finally give in.

A moment later my eyes rip open, recalling that I bought Tyler an engagement ring today. Kurat! Exhausted, I instantly fall back asleep.

Perhaps it's the traveling, or my mini emotional tsunami from earlier, but it's hard to wake up from such deep sleep. I'm a bit disoriented when I turn in bed, realizing there's a warm, hard body next to mine. First, I yelp, then I zoom in my vision on Tyler's sweet smile. He's lying on his side, head propped on his elbow, happy eyes on me.

"Sleep well?"

My brows bunch with confusion. "Where are we?" I send the room a cursory glance.

"Vegas, baby." The power of his smile grows with the appearance of his dimple.

I send a hand to touch said dimple. Because, who knows, with the performance of my mental clarity today, I better check if this Tyler is real. This Tyler is very much real, and very much amused.

"Who's with Jeremy?" I scold.

And The Smile? Grows and grows. "You care about my son more than anything, ah? Melena's with him," he says, looking at me with utter adoration. Tyler grabs my face from both sides and plants a kiss on my mouth. "Christ, I fucking love you."

"What time is it?"

"Around ten."

Utterly startled, I ask, "How did you get in?"

Tyler takes my hand and brings it to his lips. He threads our fingers together. "I persuaded the nightshift receptionist to give me a key, told him you're my girlfriend and that I wanted to surprise you. Let's just say that the fact that he's a fan didn't hurt."

"So, he just gave you a key to my room?" I frown.

"Yeah. Right after, I gave him hell about giving me the key and that he should never do that again." He smiles at me.

"Hold up. Wait a moment. How ... what?" I look at him still somewhat bewildered. "What are you doing here?"

"What?" He grins at me. "Just taking care of the *your missing-me-so-much* predicament, Kiisu." His twinkling eyes caress me. "How? Ever heard of the Wilbur and Orville brothers and they're great invention?"

"Wilbur and who?" I'm a bit confused, still in waking up mode, still absorbing the idea of Tyler here in the hotel with me.

Tyler's grin is becoming seriously hazardous to my poor smitten heart. "Wright brothers?"

"Oh, wow, Mr. Adams, dabbling in comedy tonight, are we?" We chuckle in unison. It's corny, and goofy and so wonderful. "How did you get here so fast?"

"It's not that fast, sleepyhead. The jet. We'll be taking off tomorrow morning."

"What about my ticket?"

Tyler rolls his eyes. "All's fine. Now that we got the transport issues out of the way, I know you really want to show me how much you missed me, right?"

The box harbouring The Ring flashes through my mind, but I push the thought away quicker than you can say "temporary insanity" and literally throw myself at my perfection of a boyfriend before I stupidly beg him to become my fiancé.

Getting out of the bath, after we've mutually showed each other how much being apart made us miss each other, and, ahem, hot to trot. I shrug on the #JBiebs shirt and dry my hair with a towel. I watch Tyler dry himself via the mirror. This man. I focus on my hair, so I don't attack him when we're still catching our breaths. "You know, I'm sort of jealous, and to be honest a little troubled by your interest in Mr. Bieber," I tease.

Securing the towel low on his hips Tyler eyes me through the mirror. "Jealous?" His dimple returns for an encore.

"Well, I don't see you making a #Ivi, have my baby shirt." I grin at him via the mirror.

Tyler takes a step to reach me. He wraps his arms around my waist, resting his chin on my shoulder. Amused eyes regard me via the mirror. "Well, problem solved. I can't wear that shirt anymore, it was confiscated. My girlfriend got jealous." He sends me a devilish grin and wink.

Twenty-Four

Tyler

When there's nowhere to run
When woes scream in my head
When I'm a step away from falling
You're there
Through the good, the bad and everything in-between
I thank my lucky stars for every look, smile and laugh
I thank my lucky stars for you

I toss the pen down to land on the tattered notepad and grab my guitar. I tilt my head to the side and close my eyes, letting my fingers run over the strings. I sway my head a little in rhythm with the tune in my head that morphs into the melody coming from the guitar. Humming, I strum. For a brief moment my mind drifts to something that has been in my thoughts since yesterday and a smile, a genuine smile, pushes my lips upward.

I'm not one to snoop nor pry into other's business. If you ask people who know me, they'll say I might be tilting toward the other side of the scale. Jay once told me I can be pretty obtuse in detecting or minding other's cues, or in paying attention to details for that matter. But, when I saw that square box on the nightstand at the hotel, it was stronger than me. I had to check why *my* girlfriend would have a jewelry box, one that I didn't give her. Not to mention the hotel stationary with the most supremely kooky scribble next to it: "To propose or not to propose that is the question," jotted at the top, underlined a few times too many.

People do weird shit in Vegas. Sure as hell, I've done some things in that city that I'm not too proud of, but this … I can't stop grinning. Ivi didn't seem hungover when she woke up. I think I can cross out an impulse, under the influence ring shopping spree. And the notes on that paper, God, it was really damn hard holding it in when I wanted to laugh so fucking hard. Her scribbled, revealing thoughts and futile attempt at erasing some of them. She's the sweetest damn human I know.

I know it's a private note, and I'm an awful person for taking a snap of the list, but it was too damn gold not to capture it for eternity.

I glance over at the gifted author of said list, having the most powerful urge to wake her up, kiss her brains out and handcuff her to me so she'll stay with me forever. This woman. I know her so well, every smile, wrinkles of joy, frowns, scent and curves, yet every time she's near me, I get this inexplicable impulse to touch her, and every time I do … the feeling is euphoric, electrifying. I let her sleep, she looks so beautiful and peaceful. She's fucking *everything*. I shake my head, a grin still plastered across my face as I pull out my phone. There are so many haphazardly written phrases and scattered words, some bold, some struck through. It's charming, chaotic and dizzying. I read them all again, pausing on the highlights, having a hard time controlling my grin.

To propose or not to propose that is the question!

'Cause I'm a good person and a loving girlfriend!!! **Yes, babe, you're the best.**

I adore Jeremy. **And I adore you tenfold for it.**

~~*Does his kind even take commitment seriously?*~~ **My kind? His kind takes you more seriously than you could ever imagine.**

Sundae!!! **I chuckle, because ... gold!**

Naeruväärne! **Yeah, Kiis, it's ridiculous, you shouldn't have even a single doubt when it comes to me.**

I'm an idiot. **Nope, hon. Just a little, adorably nutty.**

Grapes? Fruit?

Should I wait for him to do that? **I'd fucking die of happiness if you asked me first.**

~~*He can have ANYONE! He could reel them in left and right.*~~ **Babe, no one other than you matter.**

Coke! With tons of ice!

Why am I even considering this? **'Cause I'm you're future, Kiis.**

Nõdrameelne **Agree. You are a little insane, but in the most awesome way possible.**

I know he loves me. **Dam right, baby. Every single word, damn right.**

Pickles!!! **This one I don't even comment at in my head, I just laugh out loud.**

CHAPTER
Twenty-Five

"Pride and love don't mix. Don't hold back. Tell me everything you got. No judgment. No Ego. Just you and me." Lyrics Tyler has been jotting down, absently playing a riff that's been on repeat in his head.

"Knock knock." I open the door to Tyler's studio, smiling in response to his inviting grin.

"What can I do you for, Kiis?" He stands to walk over to me. Reaching me, he tips to touch my lips in a light kiss. "You sure you don't want to join me tomorrow? You once told me you had a crush on the guy. You'll be able to meet him in person." Tyler teases me about meeting the Tonight Show host. Once, I said he was cute, more like my runner up in celebrity crushes, but hey, I got my first, so who needs seconds?

I shake my head, keeping my hand with what I'm holding behind my back and send the other to his waist, pulling him a little closer. "I have a date with someone far more important to watch the show."

"That so?" Knowing full-well that I'm talking about Jeremy, Tyler still continues with our little flirt session.

"Speaking of the kid." I slide my hand under his shirt. "We should get going soon. Honestly, I really think Melena could use some time away from the hospital, especially now that Jeremy is making such a good recovery."

Tyler leans in to nuzzle his lips against my ear. "Concur."

Closing my eyes, enjoying every soft kiss and the feel of his scruff against my skin, I say, "Before we go, there was something I wanted to give you."

Tyler's lips freeze for a beat against my skin. He straightens to his full height, eyes searching mine. There's a new quality about him, he seemed anxious albeit in a pleasant sort of way. As if he's expecting something, good news, maybe. He swallows, his eyes round in tenderness. "What is it?"

I give him a curious look and dismiss reading oddness in his reaction. "Well, it's something I wanted to give you because — " I tilt my head assessing his physical response. I swear, I'm not imagining things. He looks … tensely eager, somewhat boyish. I'm not sure what's causing him to act this way, but whatever it is, it's beyond sweet. I spontaneously giggle, making Tyler mirror me with a nervous chuckle. Weird, but I want to record this moment so I can watch it on repeat.

As I bring my hand from behind my back, Tyler's lips stretch. If I didn't know better, I'd say his cheeks are taking a rosier shade. When he finally sees the rectangular package I'm holding, for a beat, his eyes squint in confusion as if he were expecting something completely different.

Tyler takes the gift from me, looks at it and starts unwrapping. I grin at him as he examines the framed photo. He chuckles, aligning our stares.

"I thought it would be perfect for your studio. An inspiration for many love songs to come."

This time his chuckle is a deeper one, his lips stretched wider. "If that's not romance, I don't know what is."

We grin at each other goofily. In my book, this is a perfect moment.

Tyler shakes his head as he takes another look at my gift. It's a double frame, on the left side there's a photo of me blowing a kiss at the camera, a photo Jeremy took. On the right, there's a quote in italic font. *Fun is over, babe, you have to leave now.* One of the first things Tyler ever said to me. A sentence I thought should to be commemorated for generations to come as the epitome of romance. Tyler's features set in a bright grin.

"True romance. Some of the greatest love stories were built on the foundation of such great opening lines," I say, making him laugh animatedly.

"You making fun of me, Kiisu?" Tyler asks, setting the framed photo on the desk.

I nod and grin, taking some steps back as Tyler walks my way. "Oh yeah, I am." I shriek when Tyler's arm snakes around my waist and I'm lifted, pressed against him.

Reaching the wall, Tyler turns me in his arms to straddle him and leans me against the hard surface. Unexpectedly his demeanor turns serious, sincere. With just a few inches separating us, mouths hovering closely, Tyler says in a gritty, low tone, "You know you can tell me anything, right? Or ask me to do anything you want me to." He pauses. "Or give me anything, never hesitate."

"Okaaay?" Should I tell him he's being weird? He just told me I could tell him anything…

"To me you could never do wrong. Anything coming from you would make me happy. Never hold back when it comes to us, okay?"

My lips form a small, inquisitive smile. "Okay, Tyler, you're being cryptically weird."

He inhales and places a soft kiss on my lips. "I'm just saying that you should never hold back with me. I always want you to do and say to me whatever's on your mind." He cocks his head, "Okay?" In tandem to my physical consent that comes as a nod, Tyler brings his mouth back to mine. I feel the press of his lips on mine, the mass of his body against me, his lips parting, his intoxicating breath meets mine.

Enigmatic conversation morphs into a passionate battle where we both enjoyably fight for domination, with our mouths, hands and bodies.

When we're both catching our labored breaths, leaning on the wall amid the pile of a chaos born by our discarded clothes, Tyler says, "I've set up a meeting for you with my lawyer tomorrow morning."

I'm too blissfully stupefied to ask why. The epiphany only comes much later when Tyler is already airborne, en route to New York.

Twenty-Six

Eli Cohen on Tyler Lee Adams for a magazine interview: He was a wild one.
And, boy, such strong personality and equal part stubbornness.
But I knew it. Right from the start, that boy had more talent and charisma in
his finger than most entertainers had in their entire bodies.
That boy always knew what he wanted, and he worked damn hard to get it,
nothing less than what he'd set his mind on.

"Essentially, it's up to you, Miss Kert. You can either take part in one of the existing ones or start your own project."

"There are quite a few." My statement is more to myself, given the gentleman presenting me with the portfolios is more than aware of their contents. "But — I mean, there are people working at these at the moment." I point at the portfolios spread on the table like a fan. "I don't want to compromise anyone's job."

"No one will be let off if that's your concern," he says, adjusting his olive tie, flattening it with the palm of his hand.

I unfold my crossed legs and push my sleeves up. "Wait, just to make sure I understand it correctly. I can either join these," I point at the folders. "Or start a new one?" The last part comes out as a hesitant question.

He nods, seeming somewhat bored with my slow comprehension.

To my defense, it's not like I'm used to getting these proposals often or *ever* for that matter. Not many people get to fulfil their dreams, not to mention have them served on a silver platter. "Exactly. Mr. Adams said to allocate half a million for a new project. I'm sure that if it'll require additional funds, it won't be a problem."

I blink at him and blink again. Perplexed, I stay silent for a whole minute, trying to wrap my head around everything Tyler's lawyer, Mr. Daniels, shared with me just now.

"Miss Kert?" Eli attempts to draw my attention. "Ivi." I turn to him, pulled out of my contemplation. "Why don't you take these," he says while collecting the folders and handing them to me. "Review them, think about what interests you. Come up with your own idea if you'd like and then set a follow up meeting with Mr. Daniels. You can take your time to decide how you'd like to proceed. No one is rushing you to make a decision."

Tyler's lawyer rises to stand. Buttoning his jacket, he pulls out a business card from his wallet and hands it to me. "I'll be expecting your call."

Long after both men leave, I stay seated on the sofa, holding the folders pressed to my chest and gaze out the window to the garden. My perplexity is an outcome of a prior misguided assumption. When Tyler mentioned the meeting, I didn't really know what to think. One of the ideas that came to mind was that Tyler wanted me to sign some sort of a living-together-agreement, a "prenup" of sorts for a so called common-law partner. Which I wouldn't have held against him considering our "scale of wealth" tilts radically to his side.

No, the meeting wasn't about that.

On the contrary, I've just been offered half a million dollars to start my own charity. Or, if I choose so, to help manage the Tyler Lee Adams Foundation or join one of the charities he's been continuously supporting. I pick up the thickest folder and leaf through it. Tyler's main project, to spread his passion for music by providing schools with needed assistance in creating exclusive music programs and scholarships for students. On the one hand, I'm surprised that I didn't know about Tyler's charitable activities thus far, at least in such detail that is, but on the other hand, Tyler is not one to brandish his achievements or his benevolent doings. I now remember somewhat vaguely Tyler telling me something about donations. On cue, my phone chimes with the man in subject on the other end. I swipe my finger on the screen and bring the device to my ear.

"I just realized something, Kiisu," Tyler says in place of a greeting.

"Tere you." I smile goofily. "What did you just realize, Tyler."

"That you don't have a nickname for me?"

Could he be any sweeter? "Who says I don't?" I grin wider. "I use it all the time … when I think of you. It actually stars in my inner dialogues."

"That so?"

"Mm-hmm."

I can hear the distinctive candor of joy in his voice when he says, "I'm all ears, Kiis."

I can't control the dose of honey that infuses my voice as I say, "Mine."

He's quiet for a moment. "I'm considering legally changing my name now," he says, prompting a giggle from my side of the line.

"So how did it go with Jace?" It takes me a moment to make the connection that Jace must be Mr. Daniel's first name.

"Well… It was quite a surprise. Not what I expected the meeting to be about, for sure." I regret putting it this way because I know it will bring up —

"What did you think he'd meet you for, then?"

Now, that's a conversation I'd rather skip. "Just, nothing. I was just surprised. I mean pleasantly surprised."

"Kiisu," his resolute voice demands. "Brutal honesty please, what was it?"

Brutal honesty. I ponder for a beat. A key to a successful relationship, or maybe a way to hurt each other with pretense of morality? I feel like the brutal aspect is a landmine, there's no good outcome of brutality, ever. "I just thought that maybe, I don't know, ahem, you — you might want me to sign a common law partner agreement." I squint my eyes, bracing for things to come.

"A what?" Tyler asks baffled. "Are you serious, right now?" He pauses. Sounding a tad more collected, he says, "You were right, some things are better left unsaid, especially if it's complete nonsense."

"Well, I'd totally understand and honestly, I'd encourage you to have me sign one."

"Ivi." Uh-oh, I've been demoted from Kiisu to Ivi. *Here we go…* "You know what? It's a shame you feel this way. What would it take for you to understand what you mean to me?"

"I'm just saying — "

Disregarding my attempt at clarifying my standpoint, Tyler asks next, "So, any idea what you want to do?"

Not a huge fan of raising a white flag, I decide to let this one go. "Not sure yet, but, thank you, I'm so grateful."

"Don't mention it. I'm more than confident that you'll do great things. Go ahead use my name, use my influence, use my money to do the magic you already do but on a larger scale because — "

"Tyler," I cut him mid-sentence. "I love you."

"Kiis, you're everything."

CHAPTER
Twenty-Seven

"Sorry ladies."
The Tonight Show host to the audience after asking
Tyler if the rumors about his love life are true.

I arrive at the hospital late at night as agreed with Melena, dropping off coffees and some baked goods (courtesy of Adina) at the nurses' station. The overworked ladies reward me with grateful smiles, a couple of tired appreciative head nods and a brief update on Jeremy's latest shenanigans. The kid, for sure, has a fan club.

I nod at the guard sitting outside Jeremy's room. No matter how much Melena, Jay and I tried to convince Tyler that Jeremy doesn't require twenty-four seven security outside his room, he wouldn't hear of it. He still carries the guilt of everything that happened to Melena and Jeremy. Surprisingly, Eli who's a constant voice of reason was on Tyler's side. I lightly knock on the door and open it. I pop my head inside, "Everyone decent?"

"Hilarious," Jeremy retorts.

I smile at Melena as I enter the room. "Here we go, a special delivery from Adina." I set the canvas bag filled to the brim with goodies on the bed. Jeremy cracks a smile as he lifts himself to an upright position, peeking inside the bag.

Jeremy murmurs appreciably, "Sweet."

Passing by me, Melena squeezes my hand, "Thanks, Ivi." She steps over to kiss Jeremy's head. "Have fun, you two."

"Us three," says Jay, entering the room. He hugs Melena before she leaves and turns to shrug off his blazer.

Jay makes his way to the large loot bag. "So, what have we got here?"

I take off my shoes, order the kid to scoot over and plant myself by his side on the bed. "Where's the remote?"

"You know we could have watched a taped one," Jay says teasingly.

I shake my head. "We're watching the live show."

"It's not even really live, it was taped earlier today," Jeremy joins Jay's reasoning.

I fold my hands. "Shush, both of you, just shush!"

I get a synchronized eye roll duet which I dismiss with a little hand wave while bringing the TV to life.

Jay kicks off his shoes, falls into an armchair by Jeremy's bed while shoving a whole fresh cinnamon roll into his mouth. Graceful.

Glancing at the mounted TV, Jeremy asks the room, "Did you know that the word Television was coined in 1900 by a Russian scientist?"

Jay and I trade a smile. "No, I didn't, but thanks for sharing," I say, navigating to the right channel.

Jeremy grins. "Did you know that before electric televisions we had mechanical ones?"

"Dude, it's on." Jay grins, tipping his chin at the device in subject.

On cue to the Tonight Show intro, the three of us fall silent, our joined attention directed at the mounted screen.

The monologue as always, leaves me with a faint smile. Relaxed, with my legs crossed before me by Jeremy's side, my smile grows as Jimmy Fallon presents his next guest. "Ladies and gentlemen, Tyler.

Lee. Adams!" Just by mentioning Tyler's name, the audience comes alive.

As Tyler steps on stage, he becomes the main focus of my attention. He's sporting a few days of stubble, his eyes slightly squinted with joy, looking everything the entertainer that he is in white crisp shirt, suspenders and plaid trousers. To vigorous clapping, Tyler takes a seat, a faint, flirtatious smile hovering over his lips.

Tyler takes a sip of the mug by his side as a response to Jimmy's mentioning of him being GQ Sexiest Man Alive. When Jimmy amicably pesters Tyler with a cheeky grin and a probing look, Tyler shakes his head. "An honor to be in such great company," he refers to a few winners from previous years Jimmy mentioned.

Letting him off the hook, Jimmy continues with, "You've been working on a new album, actually two projects."

"Yeah, the soundtrack for a movie, *Hearts*, together with Brooklyn Mars and Dante and some new material in the making." I rub the charm of my necklace with Tyler's name on it between my finger and thumb, full-heartedly beaming at the screen. Tyler bobs his head, confirming that both the movie and the soundtrack release date mentioned by the host as he brings up the soundtrack's cover art for a camera close-up.

"A lot of things happening to you. Congrats on the VMA award." Jimmy turns back to Tyler. Tyler nods modestly. Jimmy's smile lifts. "And," He clears his throat somewhat theatrically. "There's a rumour going around that Tyler Lee Adams is off the market?"

With a cheeky tight lip smile Tyler nods in affirmation.

Jimmy puts his hand behind his ear, pretending to listen. "Can you hear that? The avalanche of hearts breaking across the world?"

Tyler chuckles, lowering his eyes humbly and reaches for the black mug once more. He takes a sip and returns to look at Jimmy.

"What, like the real deal?" Jimmy insists with a huge grin.

Tyler's dimple makes its debut for tonight. "The real deal, Jim."

Jimmy's brows lift up. Tyler nods, lips trapping a smile. With his hand, Jimmy gestures for Tyler to go on. "The real deal?"

Tyler's grin lets loose. "I'm talking Tom Cruise circa 2005 jumping on Oprah's couch — real."

Jimmy chuckles, giving Tyler a mischievous grin. Tyler's eyes crinkle at the sides in return. "Dude, you know I need to ask you to do that now. The sofa jumping thing."

Tyler throws his head back with a chuckle. He shakes his head with humor.

Matching Tyler's amusement, Jimmy says, "Dude." He gestures at the sofa imitating a jump by curving his hands.

Tyler sends two fingers to hover over his upper shirt's button with a teasing smile. "Umm, how about I strip for you instead, Jim?"

"Wha?" Jeremy shrieks next to me. "What is he doing?"

Hugging a pillow to my chest I bite on my lips. *What is he doing?*

Jimmy turns to the band, "We need special music, here." The tune to Put Some Sugar on Me fills the stage.

Sporting the most mischievous side smile, slowly, Tyler moves on to the next button. Yells and whistles follow from the audience. As Tyler's fingers move lower, Jimmy feigns fanning himself with the notecards. Reaching the last button, Tyler rips his shirt open to reveal a plain white tee decaled in black letters across the front with "#Ivi, have my baby."

First, my jaw drops. Then, to the close-up on Tyler's smile, not only my lips stretch, but my entire face turns into one, huge crimson smile.

"Hold up, does this mean I'm going to have a little brother or a sister?" Jeremy points at the screen, looking at me hopefully.

I blink at him. "What? No." My brows pinch. "I mean — " I swallow hard. "I mean, not now, or."

Jay's chuckle is like a life buoy, lifting me up from my own deep confusion. "He's just joking." I finally tell Jeremy. *Here you go, Ivi, you finally got your own "have my baby" shirt. But for the love of God Tyler, on TV, in front of God knows how many people?*

Just before the interview is concluded, Tyler blows me away once more, this time by telling Jimmy about my new project, giving it wider exposure. Jay sends me a gentle look which I counter with pinched brows, communicating a genuine swoon over my one and only. "Sleeping pods for homeless people," Tyler explains and Jimmy nods. "The wooden pods provide a mattress and storage space and have curtains for privacy. Most importantly, they offer security and shelter."

Sleeping pods for homeless people in L.A., that's the project I chose to start in addition to my volunteering at YWPO. A project that with Tyler's name and connections didn't take too long to raise attention and funding. The people I managed to reach using Tyler's name. My jaw literally dropped when the mayor pledged a hefty sum a year in additional help to the sleeping pods. But no matter how busy I am with the project, I decided to keep volunteering at YWPO, especially the field work. There's a lot to be said about bringing projects to life that help people. Running it, raising donations, bringing an idea to an actual operating program. However, to me, nothing compares to hands on manual work, to interacting with the actual humans you help.

"You know what I just realized?" Jeremy asks, bringing me back from my thoughts.

I turn to him.

Appearing pensive, Jeremy says, "You're going to be my stepmom."

I'm not sure what my expression transpires, but I can only imagine it's not of the cool variety, what with the elated chuckle coming from Jay. I throw him a glare.

"What?" Jay asks over a chuckle. "The man just wore a shirt

declaring he wants you to have his baby on the God damn Tonight Show."

Hesitantly, my eyes go back to Jeremy, only to find a full-blown smarty-pants smile radiating my way.

Twenty-Eight

"When all the pieces fit together,
a jigsaw puzzle produces a complete picture."
Instructions for a jigsaw puzzle Jeremy and Ivi completed earlier together.

I jump up from the lounger to get the tray Adina is carrying. "I was planning on coming in to get some snacks soon, you really didn't have to," I tell Adina, sending my hands forward for the tray.

Passing by me with a dainty smile, Adina whispers, "It's my job, honey, when will you get used to it? And, I enjoy doing it."

Right. I'm well aware of that. But still, I guess it is an innate thing, or the way I was brought up. I can't have someone older than me attend to me in such a way. Probably will never get used to it either.

Shadowing his eyes with his hand, Tyler sends me a humoured gaze. "Thanks Adina," he says to Adina as she sets a tray with fruits and lemonade on the low table. His eyes return to me for a wordless conversation.

His: It's her job.

Mine: I don't care. She could be my mom; I'd never have my mom run around for me.

His: Get your sweet ass over here, sit next to me.

Mine: Happily.

"Wow, you just totally neuron mirrored him," Jeremy declares as my rear hits the lounger, taking a seat next to Tyler.

I squint at the kid and turn to the dad person. "What did I just do to you?" I question Tyler who shrugs animatedly in return. I turn back to Jeremy, "I neuroed what?"

Clever brown eyes do a full-fledged roll from under blue glasses. In a bored tone, kept to dealing with the less gifted, Jeremy says, "You know how there are three types of communication, right?"

Both Tyler and I nod, watching him closely, albeit with identical amused smiles. Tyler squeezes my thigh. Jeremy explains, "It's like you guys have the nonverbal one down pat. You even copy each other's gestures." Returning to his bored tone, he turns back to me and adds, "Neuron mirroring is when the neuron of an animal or a human 'mirrors' the behavior of another human or animal, as if the observer were itself acting."

"How about you neuron mirror yourself doing your homework?" Tyler says, imitating Jeremy's flat tone.

I smile at Jeremy as he reluctantly retrieves a notebook and a pencil case from his gamers' backpack. It's so nice having him back home, as if everything simply fell back into place. Melena is in a meeting out of town, so Jeremy stays with us tonight. It's almost ridiculous how everyone spoils him rotten since his release from the hospital. From Adina, to Tyler, Jay, me and even Eli. And the kid? Soaking it up like a happy, little, overindulged, bespectacled sponge.

Utterly content, I slide to lie on my side next to Tyler, resting my head on his chest, the one adorning the #Ivi have my baby shirt. Also known as my favorite shirt on the planet. Needless to say, I raised my displeasure with Tyler when he came back home for choosing to debut our little joke shirt on none other than The Tonight Show. That little show with roughly eleven million viewers. His response was kissing me stupid till I nearly forgot my mother tongue.

"The shirt," Jeremy peeps from beside us. Tyler pivots to look at him while I raise a sleepy head, squinting one eye under the illuminating sun. "Is it, like, a wooing thing or a hint for things to come."

Takes me a minute to make sense of the things to come part, to which I immediately respond. "A private joke." My words colliding with Tyler's "Both."

With my mouth parted, I gape at Tyler.

He cocks his head, reciprocating my baffled stare with an easygoing one. I squint Jeremy's way, confirming the kid has lost his interest in us and whisper. "Both? What?"

Grinning, Jeremy loudly whispers, "You know I'm sitting right here, I can clearly hear your whisper, Ivi." Smugly, the kid air quotes "whisper."

Tyler chuckles utterly amused by the entire situation.

I let it go.

———————— ◆ ————————

It's been a long day. A rarely, blissfully quiet day. It's not too often that we spend an entire day together, the three of us, Tyler, Jeremy and me. With Tyler's constant traveling, meeting, practicing and generally work filled days, together with the time I invest on the Sleeping Pods project, mainly looking to expand it to other cities and my time with YWPO, we don't get much quality time together. So, when days like this come by, especially with Jeremy back home, I indulge in having them both by my side to the fullest.

Brushing my teeth, I think about the lovely evening we've just spent with pizza and a movie and snuggling by the fire. I don't need more than this. This is perfect.

"Hey Kiis," Tyler says, entering the en suite. "So now we're neuron mirroring each other."

I smile at him. "We've reached a new level in our relationship."

"I've never neuron mirrored with anyone else before," Tyler murmurs. My smile stretches. "Kiis, this is serious material, right here. I don't think that many relationships can top this." And my smile grows bigger and bigger. A wicked, wicked grin prompts his dimple to sink deep as he tears off his shirt, pulling it up over his head. "How about you neuron mirror me, right now?"

Rinsing my mouth, I turn to look at him. I squint my eyes and cock my head, tilt it back and with enough attitude as if I own this game, I get rid of my shirt. Tyler stares at me as I stand before him with a baby pink lace bra, boy shorts and fluffy, wool socks up to my knees.

He shakes his head, murmuring, "Damn."

Sparks fly wild between us as Tyler slowly steps my way. I watch him, realizing, all the pieces of my life are falling into place. My career, my wellbeing, my place in this world, it's all getting together. And him, Tyler, the last piece that completes this puzzle into a picture of a promising, exciting future.

CHAPTER
Twenty-Nine

CHAPTER

"Ivy Who? Brooklyn Mars and Tyler Lee Adams Spend Thanksgiving
Together at Tyler's L.A. Mansion."
Tabloid headlines quoting a source "close" to the "couple."

"You look nice," Jeremy throws my way just before skipping down the stairs way too fast to be safe.

"Thanks," I say to his back. "Jer, be careful! You're still recovering, you could — " and he's gone, joining the large group of joyful voices congregated in the main living room. By his behavior you can't tell what the kid went through merely a month ago. Holding the banister, I lean forward to catch a glimpse of everyone. Everyone, a medley of people closest to Tyler and me. From Jay, Eli, and Melena to Brooklyn, Dottie and even my parents who Tyler flew over to spend Thanksgiving with us, with me.

Yesterday when I opened the door to their familiar, loving faces I nearly lost my ability to form words. The surprise, the excitement and love left me speechless. Apparently, Tyler managed to convince my parents, who rarely leave their hometown, to fly across the world to spend some time with us. When I asked Tyler how he'd managed to communicate with them, given their very limited English and Tyler's nonexistent Estonian, he just shrugged and dismissed it with a simple, "Where there's a will there's a way, Kiis."

With a ridiculously happy sigh, I run my hand over my little A-line, black dress, smoothing it before taking the steps down. I pass by the kitchen first, check if Adina needs any help, which she declines with a feign scowl that follows by a calm smile, whispering, "You go on, honey, people are waiting for you."

Taking a seat between my dad and Tyler, I do a double take when my eyes meet Max. Pointing at Max, I lean a little toward Tyler, asking, "Have I met this one before?"

Tyler chuckles in response. "Weird, ah?"

"Just weird? I'm more than a little uncomfortable." I eye the person in subject doubtfully. "Do you think he'll, I don't know, go through some scary transformation if he's exposed to light, or fed after midnight?"

Tyler's lips stretch wider at my insinuation that Max is a cute little mogwai that might transform into an evil gremlin soon. Because, the version of Max sitting across the table is new to me, all cleaned up and sweet, hair slicked and combed back. It's unsettling to say the least.

"Wait till you see how he acts next to the likes of," Tyler gestures with a circle hand movement around the room and then nods toward the entrance where just like magic, with a soft throat clearing sound, enters a mousey, slender lady in a pink sundress. A sweet, summery, teenage targeted perfume advertisement jumps to my mind as a reaction to young, rosy-cheeked, nerdy Gwyneth Paltrow lookalike. My lips part to Max, clumsy and hesitant, pushing back from his chair, the top of his cheeks tint.

A little baffled, I turn to Tyler. To my wordless question, Tyler just nods with a tipped lip, communicating "Told ya."

"Now I've seen it all." I murmur.

Tyler chuckles beside me, leaning in to press a kiss on my temple.

"I guess when a cute girl is involved sometimes a leopard does change its spots."

Still rather incredulous to this oddest of transformations, I ask, "And what, loses his spots and turns into a Chihuahua?"

The dinner is a lovely chaotic affair, what with the number of people around the table, talking to each other, over each other and in groups. Jeremy is being extra sweet, trying to entertain my parents with the help of a translation app. Jay and Killer, plotting a boy only trip to wherever to which Melena shakes her head my way, animatedly rolling her eyes. Dad surprisingly looks more than comfortable in this diverse surrounding. Mom seems blissful, sipping at her champagne, her fond, full gaze sweeping the room. Brooklyn and her girlfriend, Bebe, safe in this welcoming environment, show each other extra affection like no one's watching. The new Max doesn't even catch a glimpse of the lovers beside him, utterly focused on his new sweet object of affection.

All in all, it's sort of odd, yet utterly perfect.

Gently tilting back with my chair, I feel almost illegally happy, floating in a bubble of sentimental joy. You rarely get to experience this kind of connection and friendship in your life. One that leaves you whole and content.

I feel Tyler's warmth as he leans closer to me. "Hey Kiis, how about you, me and a lifetime of this?"

I slowly turn to him with a wide smile, tilted back, still balancing on two legs of the chair. "Yes. So much yes."

His eyes shine at me. "Okay then, I guess I'll do it properly, get the ring and all."

Get the ring and all? That's when I lose my balance on the chair and ever so not elegantly fall back with the silliest of shrieks. At first, Tyler's hand flies out to catch me, his features crumbled with worry. He manages to catch my hand and eases the landing impact. He assesses me for a frozen beat. When he realizes that I'm good, no real injuries in sight, he traps the smile stretching his lips with his teeth, and all urgency vanishes.

Tyler leaves his seat and dropping down to his haunches, he whispers, "You okay?"

I nod, rosy warmth taking over my cheeks.

"Kallis, kas olete koras?" My mom's concerned voice from a couple seats away sobers me a little.

"Kõik hea, ema," I'm fine, I answer, eyes glued to the man who just made me lose my balance. Figuratively and literally.

Eyes crinkled adorably at me, Tyler cocks his head. Still whispering, he adds, "Is it just me, or does it seem like each time I declare my love for you, you end up falling on your ass?"

I let out a spontaneous giggle. "Maybe it's time I do the declarations, you know, just to avoid further unnecessary injuries."

His grin at me grows brighter and brighter. "Fucking crazy about you," he whispers. Sending his hand to my waist, Tyler helps me to my feet.

Warring my lips, my own words thunder in my head, "Maybe it's time I do the declarations." My heart is about to bang its way out of my chest as I raise on my tiptoes to whisper next to Tyler's ear, "Come with me upstairs?"

A cheeky grin touches Tyler's lips. "I'm always down with *going with you upstairs*, but now? With all of our guests here?"

For a millisecond my brows pinch. "Not that kind of come with me upstairs." The thrill that left me for a beat returns when I say, "I just need to talk to you, alone, okay?"

Tyler observes me hesitantly then mumbles some excuse to the room with a reason I don't even hear given my mind is spinning, and follows me up the stairs.

Tyler's smile morphs into a quizzical one when I pass the bed and lead him to our joined dressing room. The question on his face only deepens when I rummage through my underwear drawer like an unhinged crazy lady. When I finally find the little velvet box and turn to him, the air between us changes drastically. I can hardly breathe due to my anxiety, seems like the same act is quite a challenge for him too when his eyes meet the box.

I squeeze the box in one hand. Tyler's eyes zoom in on the gesture. I clear my throat, not that it helps any. My voice still comes out graveled when I say, "I love you." Tyler's emotional eyes adhere to mine. "So incredibly much." When his lips part to speak, I raise my free hand to lightly press two fingers on his lips. "Don't say anything, please. Just leave it out there for a moment." I repeat in a shaky voice, "I love you."

Following my request, Tyler stays quiet. However, what transpires from his face assures me that I'm doing the right thing.

Swallowing over the emotions in my throat, I open my hand to reveal the box. "Would you — " I swallow once more as my entire being is treading through an immense wave of apprehension. I take a deep breath, "Would you be my hus — my forever?"

Tyler doesn't say a word. Instead he brings both his hands to cup my cheeks. For a silent beat he looks at me with enough sentiments to melt my core. Slowly, ever so slowly, he brings his lips to mine for the softest of kisses. Next, he doesn't hug me, he wraps his arms around me to swallow me complete. Resting his lips on the crown of my head he finally says heavy with feelings, "*Nothing* I want more."

For an overwhelming stretch we remain wrapped up in each other and then our lips meet. Slow and gentle and transcendentally perfect.

Epilogue

Tyler
2 weeks later

I send a finger to the phone's screen held in Jeremy's palm; with just a little force I slightly push it down — for sake of attention. The kid's eyes, somewhat unfocused, look up from the device. "It's about to start," I say, and he nods. First time in *never* that my son doesn't show displeasure or provide a long list of supporting facts or, hell, a full-on closing argument before switching off a game. Who said miracles don't happen?

Try as I might to blend in, I still get more than a couple of curious looks, and some not so surreptitious phone cameras directed my way. I cringe. Not what I wanted. Nevertheless still saw it coming. It's not about me. I'm just a spectator today. It's entirely about my Ivi who trades hesitant glances between the guy on the stage who's about to introduce her to the audience and me. I send her a reassuring smile, communicating, "You got this, babe." Because I know she'll absolutely slay it. She's Ivi, after all.

Her first couple of steps are tentative. Her timid air throws me back to Thanksgiving eve. Never have I felt so overwhelmed and flabbergasted by someone. I wasn't a stranger to that box with the ring. We spent more than a few humored and wistful moments in Vegas together just before I put it away, never even implying I knew of its existence. But, Christ, when Ivi pulled it out with every intention to ask me to be hers, I was a goner.

Ivi seems to take a deeper, reassuring breath, squares her shoulders and makes her way to the center of the stage with enough charisma and grace to make my proud smile stretch wider. She adjusts the wireless mic, timidly smiling at the audience. She sends me a stolen glance and starts. "Funny, most of you know me, not for who I am but for being linked to someone else. So, maybe I'll start by introducing myself." It's a rocky beginning but soon she captures them entirely, delivering her speech passionately with just enough intrigue to keep her listeners attentive.

Ivi goes on, "My, our relationship, is a home, not a billboard."

I couldn't agree more. Seamlessly, she segues to the real subject she's here to talk about. I space out, not sure for how long. I'm lost. Completely lost. Her perfect eyes are all that I can see. I sober up to a wave of laughter and clapping. My feelings for her tantalize me, not for what she just said, or this Ted Talk she is delivering, but for everything she is. For the multitude of emotions and pride buzzing through me toward her.

I give Jeremy a sidelong glance. His brows are pinched. He slightly nods, agreeing with Ivi's words about public shaming.

Rewarding the audience with a semi-frustrated smile, Ivi says, "These permissive environments seeding hate and humiliation, where we are told, or hinted at how we should look, what we should wear, how we should talk, think, and feel to fit in." Captivated, both Jeremy and my attention are trained on her. "But you have a choice, you can choose not to let people out there attack you in the safety of your own home, or do that to others. Chose who to follow and unfollow, and most of all, give people on social media the same courtesy and respect you'd give them in real life. We all need to remember that words hurt, words affect, sometimes words can be deadly even when they're delivered via a keyboard."

Ivi pauses for a few beats, letting her message absorb. She then sends the audience a timid smile. "I never wanted to be in the spotlight but since I've practically been dragged into it, as you may know, I thought I might as well use it for a good cause. All benefits tonight go to YWOP."

"Soon I'll be known for being Ivi Kert's boyfriend," I tease Ivi who sits astride me on the bed, wearing my shirt, her favorite #Ivi-have-my-baby one and wool socks up to her knees. Looking as stunning as ever, casual and face free of makeup. Pure and natural is my favorite version of Ivi. Since the moment I got to know her, she changed the conversation inside my head, tweaking it, boosting it, spicing it little by little as she, little by little got under my skin. Slowly and persistently made her way into my heart till she owned it completely. I thought back then that I had it all figured out, was on the top of the world, living the life. Little did I know just how much was missing to make me feel genuinely complete. Ivi opened my eyes to what I was missing. In a subtle way it was Ivi who first guided me on how to reach my own child. She was there, silently yet influentially showing me how to get closer, how to open up, how to stop second guessing every move I made. Stop regretting the past and embrace the future. And eventually, how to fall completely and insanely in love.

"You mean Ivi Kert's fiancé," she friendly smacks my abs, her fingers linger, not so sneakily copping a feel. "Soon *I* will be known as

Ivi Kert-Adams." Here she goes, killing me again.

"If that's not the most fucking beautiful thing I've ever heard." And I get the sweetest kiss. Killing me, little by little.

Ivi slowly leans back from our kiss. To the rhythmic tapping sound of rain. She tilts her head up to the skylight ceiling. A soft smile takes over her face. Contemplating, she murmurs, "It's December again."

"Tis," I say, slowly dragging my open palms up her thighs. When her eyes are back on me, I say, "Just a year ago you were getting me spiked on eggnog, with your little cute outfit, all 'Tyler kiss me, Tyler kiss me.'"

Her eyes grow. "What?" She shakes her head, puffing out feigned frustration. "You were the one who started it all."

"Excuse me." I muster innocence. "Me?" Unable to hold it in, my lips pull up devilishly. "Who came up to my room and practically forced me to have dinner with her?"

I get a friendly smack to my chest. "You're incredible. Forced?"

"Not to mention tried to sedate me with poisonous food just to have her wicked way with me?" I let out a smug chuckle.

"Hey, that's slander!" Her nose wrinkles animatedly.

"Whatever," I laugh. My grin? Grows and grows. She's fucking sweet.

"And you know how litigious I can get." She cocks her head, challenging me.

My fingers slide under her shirt, slowly rising toward her ribs, leaving goosebumps in their wake. "I better get on your good side then." I trail my fingers higher, Ivi's lips part, humor gone, replaced by heat. For a brief moment I feel this pang to my chest. The knowledge of how much she wants me sends me to places so far beyond the realm of logic and control. The burn in me goes wild as I slowly strip her of her clothes. And when I finally sink into her, the feeling — it takes my breath away.

I've never met someone like her. I'm still in awe of her. Someone as selfless. Someone one who's goal in life is to give back. We're all too cynical. Ivi, on the other hand, truly believes that we can make this world a better place. She's definitely made my world damn better, in every sense.

Epilogue

Jeremy
2 weeks later

"Aaand this one's for you." I retrieve an envelope from under the decorated tree, handing it to Ivi who's still in her white night shirt and knee-length green and red stripy socks pushed up to her knees. Ivi is sitting crossed legged next to me, leaning her back against my dad's bare chest. She takes the envelope from my hand with a sleepy, content smile. Okay, I may have woken them a bit early. Okay, it might have been way too early. In my defence, it is Christmas morning. They didn't really expect me to wait for the presents, did they? I mean, duh.

"Tyler told me everything." I grin, thinking about how creative my gift is. "Every little detail about the two of you last Christmas eve," I say by way of explanation. My brows knit and I adjust my glasses up my nose with my pointer finger as I observe her reaction. My frown deepens, she looks a little sick all of a sudden. Ivi is pale-ish as she turns with a horrified expression to look at my dad.

Seeing Ivi's face, my dad tilts his head backward with a laugh. He brings his hand to cover his eyes, still chuckling, he murmurs, "This is gold." Seeming unable to contain his amusement, he adds, "You should have seen your face, Kiis."

"Tyler… seriously. You told him… *everything*?" Ivi stammers. "Seriously?" Her tone is harsher this time.

I'm having a hard time following whatever just happened. Adults can be so weird sometimes. Especially Ivi and my dad; sometimes they have these ridiculous conversations that no one really gets. It's as if half of the data transferred between them is encrypted. Like they have their own language. Whatever.

"What?" Tyler asks over a chuckle. "The kid's trying to give you something."

Tentatively Ivi turns back to me. She clears her throat. "I guess I'm going to find out what's inside," she murmurs half to herself.

Before she manages to completely unwrap the gift certificate, I hurry and say, "Tyler said you cooked the worse dinner ever last Christmas that nearly killed him." I grin at her. "Cooking lessons! Booyah!"

My dad's grin is almost blinding. I guess he appreciates the brilliant idea.

"Thanks Jer, very thoughtful," Ivi moves over to hug me. When she takes her place back between dad's thighs, she throws him a stink eye. Adults … And according to science teenagers' neurons are still only half-baked. Go figure.

It's my turn now. BOOYAH! They shower me with gifts. It's a known fact that a spoiled kid may be unwilling to conform to ordinary demands. I'm keeping this little nugget to myself. Because … presents! Dad and Ivi watch me with matching smiles, yeah, they get those a lot when they observe me or when I say something they find amusing. Mmhmm, weird. But I'm not going to lie, I like it. It makes me feel special. Especially the ones coming from my dad.

Wrapping paper flies around as I tear through my gifts, grinning like its Christmas morning. See what I just did there?

Sitting there surrounded by my bounty, I half listen to the conversation beside me. "Ooh, I'm coming with, right? Can I?"

"Of course," Ivi smiles at me. Again, the smile with the pride sparkle. "Sure, I'd love that. There's always a need for some extra hands. You just need to check in with your mom first. If she's fine with it, I'll pick you up six-ish, okay?" I get to go home later and open presents with my mom. Having two homes isn't a bad thing, I tell ya. I nod, happy I can go with Ivi to help over at the soup kitchen this evening.

The box left under the tree catches my eye and I cough, trying to get my dad's attention. It's something for Ivi that he promised we'd give her together since I helped in choosing it. He's too absorbed in Ivi. She isn't even talking yet he looks at her like she's about to reveal the conclusion of the Avengers Endgame movie. I cough/say into my hand "Tyler."

They both turn to me. I look at dad and then pointedly at the box. Tyler's lips tip and Ivi grins at my "sneaky" ways. Tyler sends his tattooed hand to the box and deposits it on Ivi's crossed legs. Ivi cranes her neck to look up at him, "Another one for me?"

Dad nods, lips in an easy smile.

"I helped wrap it," I say, scratching my cheek. I'm excited about this one. "And I helped choose it!"

Ivi smiles at me. "Whatever it is, I already love it." When she opens the large-ass box just to find a much, much smaller box inside, I snicker. Yup, that was my idea. Ivi sends me another grin and shakes her head, amused. When she tears off the wrapping of the smaller one, her face turns emotional. Ivi observes the blue-ish, umm, is it really blue? Maybe greenish-blue? Dunno. Okay, it's a Tiffany's box, that I know cause I've done some research. No, I don't really care about diamonds unless it's in Minecraft, but yeah, you'll get it soon, I promise.

Trapping her lip with her teeth, she turns slowly to look at my dad who's still holding her from behind. "Open it, Kiis," his voice matches her sentimental expression.

When she finally pops it open, I chime in, "It's a certified ethically sourced diamond!" See, I've done my research! "Did you know that improper diamond mining can lead to soil erosion and strip the soil of its natural nutrients? And soil erosion actually contributes to deforestation." I move my glasses up my nose, my words come out faster as I go on. "Dust and water pollution are also side effects of unsustainable diamond mining. And don't forget the human factor! The miners are grossly underpaid, while they work in extremely dangerous conditions." I'm so riled up at this point that, "And don't forget child labor!" comes out quite loud.

"Jer was the one who suggested to look for an ethically sourced diamond," my dad says, winking at me. "He did all the research."

"I can see that." Ivi moves her free hand to cover mine. "I love it, and I love the idea that you put so much thought into choosing an ethically sourced one for me. It means a lot, and it makes it all the more special to me. Thanks Jer."

When Ivi's eyes go back to the ring with the largest purple stone, her eyes mist over. She half turns in my dad's lap to look at him. "It's so special and beautiful. I love it, Tyler."

"I wanted to get you something as unique as you are." He looks at her like she's the most special thing in the universe. "Can I put it on you?"

If these two were a cartoon we'd probably have little red hearts floating around the room. When they tilt toward each other and kiss, I cringe. Seriously, don't people come up for air? When I make retching sounds, they pull apart with easy chuckles. Dad gives me a feigned death stare. I shrug and he grins at me.

"Now," Dad says. "There's this last thing, it's not exactly a tangible gift, but I think it'll make you no less happ — "

"Oooh, can I, please?" I cut him off mid-sentence. I'm so excited about this one, I can hardly wait to tell Ivi! When I plead with puppy dog eyes, he shakes his head once again. Dad gives me a small smile and gestures with his hand for me to go ahead. I grin at Ivi, she smiles back, looking at me like she really likes me. "Like Da — Tyler said, it's not exactly a present, but, urr, we think it'll make you happy. Very happy! Like, I'm talking extremely, winning a million dollars, happy!"

"Jer," Dad stops me with a hint of a smile. "She gets it, happy. Let's get to the point, shall we?"

"Da — Tyler." In my head Tyler is dad, and I love him, but sometimes, I don't know what it is, calling him dad to his face is a bit weird. Usually kids have their entire life to practice saying dad, it comes naturally. Not such a long while ago he was Tyler Lee Adams, a super famous singer and, like, overnight he became my father. Well, I know it's been over a year now, but hey, I'm getting there. "D — ad has been working with some people in Nepal. Umm, you know, social workers." Ivi frowns as she listens to me. "Those people who help kids," I add.

"Jer," it's Dad again, smiling at me. "I think Ivi knows what social workers do." He raises his brows, encouraging me to get to the point.

"So, like I said, he's been working with people in Nepal to help that kid that you really like and talk about all the time, Raj."

Ivi's eyes widen, her mouth forms an O shape.

"By helping Raj, Jeremy means that we're working on getting him adopted by some family here in the US, far from everything he went through," my dad explains.

This time Ivi's eyes don't just mist over, a real tear slides down her cheek. "Oh," her hand lands on her mouth. "Tyler, that's — " She seems too overwhelmed to go on.

Oh! I get so giddy, having an eureka moment. I blurt out next, "Why someone else, why don't you guys adopt him?"

They both turn to me with puzzled looks, and then at each other. Slowly, their expressions as though synchronized turn into similar cryptic confused smiles accompanied by a thoughtful frown. It goes on for a few good moments.

Annnd, they're at it again … having one of those wordless conversations. I swear, these two have the neuron mirroring thing down to a science.

Epilogue

Ivi
a year later

"When there's nowhere to run
When woes scream in my head
When I'm a step away from falling
You're there
Through the good, the bad and everything in-between
I thank my lucky stars for every look, smile and laugh
I thank my lucky stars for you."

Tyler sings, his voice gruff and smoky, penetrating my core, just as it does to the rest of the fourteen thousand something people singing along to his voice.

It's the last day of his recent tour that's been going on for some long few months. I missed him greatly when he was away. We all did. I decided to join him for the last week. It's the concluding show. Tonight, after this show we're going home, together. In a couple of hours, we'll head back, close the door behind us and go back to being a normal family. As "normal" as life with Tyler can be. In the past year things have fallen into place with a few highs and lows, all worth every second of it. It's been a bumpy ride having Raj adjust to his new life, to our unconventional family.

At first, I was petrified, excited yet anxious about not failing him. But Tyler was there to dismantle my concerns and insecurities. His faith in me brought and still brings me the courage to accept the fact that together, we can do it. With him by my side, on my side, sometimes I feel like there's nothing I can't do. Adopting Raj was nothing like taking care of Jeremy, Raj was my sole responsibility, mine and Tyler. We knew we'd have to help him build trust, trust in us and the rest of the world that thus far gave him none of that sort of reassurance and confidence. Albeit in baby steps, slowly he opened up to us, accepted us. Jeremy had an integral part in helping Raj adapt to his new life. The kid assumed the big brother role as I knew he would and made Raj feel nothing but welcomed and loved.

My heart squeezes at the small, big and significant moments we've shared together that eventually made us a little family. I smile, remembering Jeremy's words from some time ago, "Can you believe it, in a year my family increased by a hundred fifty percent, that's nutso!" Wild indeed, but so amazingly grand. This family, biological and chosen, this is it. It's everything.

The music winds down slowly to both Tyler and Max, sitting on stools, their heads dipped, looking at their fingers strumming the cords while Killer accompanies them with slow brush strokes on the drums. As the final notes dissolve into the buzzing venue, Tyler leans down to grab a bottle of water. He takes a long swig and adjusts the standing microphone. He sends the audience a tease of a smile, clears his throat next and the hall silences in anticipation. "You know, these songs," he tilts his head, contemplating, "they come from somewhere deep inside. When they take form on paper, they start making sense. They become something meaningful, telling your story, my story." He sends Killer a look over his shoulder with a hint of a smile. Killer nods in agreement.

Tyler's eyes move on to Max who nods, his head somewhat tilted. "Our stories." He takes another drink of water. "This one tells the story of wild nights, past mistakes and absolution." The crowd drink up Tyler's words as I do, mesmerized. "You might know this one. It's called *Unspoken Words*." And the audience roars with excited affirmation.

A reporter for the *Rolling Stones* by the name of Ron Stern wrote a review of one of the first shows of the tour that stuck with me, and having seen the show a few good times in the past week, I couldn't agree more with Mr. Stern. He couldn't have put it better. "Tyler Lee Adams — Unplugged Tour. Visually, it's a low-key spectacle; musically, it's superb," Ron wrote. "We get a more mature Tyler Lee Adams. Pure and strong but also delicate enough to expose all the finer particulars of his performance, which is exactly what you want when you're listening to one of the best musicians out there stripping everything back. The set list was sublime, with an ideal balance of new and old. The kind of show you'll remember for years to come."

Tyler Lee Adams, stripping everything back is my favorite version of my Tyler. The one I get to go to sleep with every night, the one I get to share a life with, the one that is one hundred percent ours, Jeremy, Raj and mine. We get the best version, Tyler unplugged.

Tonight, this show in particular, is more special to me. Tonight, I get to experience it like every other fan. I insisted I be able to watch the show from the audience not from behind the stage, or from the comfort of some back room. I'm standing in the front row nearest to the stage next to Jay and a date he brought with him tonight. Jay, me and Tyler's hardcore fans, those who waited since the doors opened a few good hours earlier. And it's spectacular, to be in the core of the excitement, the center of the electricity.

The crowd can't seem to get enough of Tyler. Even though it's a toned-down, acoustic show, when Tyler and the guys say goodnight and head backstage the fans go wild, chanting his name like an incantation. And when they get what they were pleading for they go even wilder. A long-ish encore later, Tyler and the guys thank the fans. Max bows while Killer lifts his drumsticks in the air, and they walk backstage. Tyler nods at the crowd and yells, "Goodnight L.A."

Instead of following Max and Killer's steps, Tyler walks to the end of the stage, bends a little and sends his hand to me. When mine is secured in his, he helps me climb up to the stage. I get a kiss on the lips to whistles and calls of excitement from an elated mass. Tyler's smile at me calls for a swarm of butterflies to go wild in my stomach.

"Can I take you home now, Mrs. Adams?" Tyler says to my ear, his voice strained and hoarse and utterly spellbinding. I nod with a soft smile and something that's so much more than just love. Tyler slides his hand across my back and into my jean pocket. I mirror him, sliding mine into his as we walk together off the stage.

Acknowledgments

THANK YOU to every single person out there who read the book!

Liis for being an inspiration for this story, and for being such a beautiful human being in general. I love you, kid.

Nicole Hornbaker, for your magnificent work and priceless suggestions. You always make the editing part so much fun.

BLOGGERS, truly incredible bloggers. I'm forever grateful and humbled by your continuous support. You are simply the best.

And last but not least, my readers. Since Layers was released, I've been constantly overwhelmed by your response. You guys are truly amazing, and I could have not asked for better readers.

A special thank you to a very special reader, the fabulous Ms. Kathy Wood Crenshaw. Tons of hugs, friend. ☺

Note from the Author

Dear Reader,

Thank you *so much* for taking the time to read Unplugged.

So, I have a request. It would be great, REALLY GREAT, actually it would be more than fantastic, if you would leave a review on Amazon, Barnes and Noble, Goodreads, or anywhere else you wish. ;-)

Also, I more than love hearing from my readers. Honestly, it's the best part of the whole writing process. So, send me an email at: author.sehrlich@gmail.com or chat with me on Facebook.

Thank you for allowing me to share my stories with you, and I hope to be re-invited to your bookshelf with my next release.

Again, THANK YOU!

Loads of x's & o's,

Sigal

Also by Sigal Ehrlich

About the Author

By her teens, Sigal had already lived in three different continents where she was lucky enough to experience and visit varied places and meet unique people, which only helped fuel her overly developed imagination. Currently, Sigal calls Prague home where she lives with her husband and three kids.

Sigal would love to hear from you! Please send her a message or visit her at:

Website: http://www.sigalehrlich.com/
Instagram: https://www.instagram.com/sigal_eh/
Twitter: @Sigal_Ehrlich
Facebook: https://www.facebook.com/sigalehrlich.author
Pinterest: http://www.pinterest.com/authorsehrlich/
Email: auhtor.sehrlich@gmail.com